Sitter

A Novel

By Larry Greer

ONE

The present story like all these phenomena called stories begins as far back as you care to go, as far back along the unbroken chain of events we call the history of everything as, say, the crazy distant day the light for even reading a story by was rewarded with a universal discharge order in the Era of Recombination (as the story of the Cosmic Microwave Background goes) for its 300,000 years spent beating its head against the wall of plasmic opacity created by the numberless electrons reveling in their freedom from the equally numberless protons bent on capturing them to form the building blocks of it all, a wall that finally gave way like the waving of a green flag at long last releasing 4×10^{84} long pent-up little instances of the ability to zip all but wheel-screechingly from zero to 670,616,629 miles per hour in any and all new things called directions in an instant or even less.

Or the present story, centered as it is (as we'll soon see) on the heartbreak of an odd phenomenon called faultiness, could quite poignantly be begun at a certain point well before the cosmos let there be light when suddenly the already-mentioned concept of defectiveness was forever inserted into the universal equation by all the literally one-in-a-billion little matter particles that were left over when the universe didn't quite get mutual matter-antimatter annihilation right.

Or of course the present story could be said to begin even further back than that along the chain of events in question, all the way back even to that earliest precursor of a thing we now call a day when in a near infinitely splittable thing we now call a second the Big Bang, as the story goes, super reverberatingly introduced the concept of beginning as the very first thing for building a universe around if you don't count the concept of nothingness whatsoever that the concept of beginning sprang from.

But let's not start that far back. Let's not even trudge all the way back to the 10.3 billion year mark of our universe's story when the already mentioned building blocks of it all pulled off the ultimately science and also philosophy-stumping miracle or magic trick of plucking a new thing called life on a newish thing a lot of us now call Earth out of thin air as we now idiomatically say four and a half billion years after air became a thing. Let's just call all the above, and an untold ton of other fundamental stuff tossed into the bargain on top of that, the backstory that tacitly informs the coming double if not triple or even quadruple love story proper.

Which I'm happy to report is starting now, or rather is starting a mere 250 million years ago at the point in spacetime where/when the already-mentioned backstory butts abruptly up against the pivotal front end (back end from our current locale in the spacetime in question) of the Triassic Period within the Mesozoic Era when a certain plodding flock of overgrown birds of the same ill-fated feather commonly known as the dinosaurs were roaming the Earth.

More specifically, there a gam's-worth if you will of these four-legged land whoppers doing their sleepy-eyed thing up there in the northwest corner of Pangea, and by doing their thing I mean they are blithely chewing their fern-cud and trying not to crush the young ones underfoot while basically amounting to nothing so much as some of the raw material for an Earth-cursing petroleum deposit that will be eons in the making once they've gone the way of all carbon-based life forms.

And yes, dear and close reader, that last paragraph was in fact a matter of your extra omniscient and poetic license-taking narrator busting the myth that it's a myth that there isn't a little bit of dinosaur in all the petroleum-based products that make our modern-day world go 'round.

TWO

And now from our story's brief opening scene in downtown Dinosaurland let's take a quantum, and I suppose also a not un-Newtonian, leap all the way to an establishing shot setting the stage for a heartbreaking scene that will soon play out (decidedly minus all the good stuff associated with the age-old behavior of playing) an even ten years before the famous "FADE OUT" comes along to mark the end of our story.

The temporal location in question is 120 years after the Lumiere brothers introduced the universe to a certain perfect complement to sticky floors and the invention of a tubful of hot buttered popcorn called the moving picture, and this they did by way of a 45-second so-called comedy (*L'Arroseur Arrose'*) all about a practical joke involving a hose and an asshole posing as a boy making life miserable for a man who only wants to water his damn garden. (Do not get your narrator started on the uncalled-for advent of practical joking in a cosmos already fraught with ways a day can go haywire.)

The reason moving pictures are important to our story is that without them and the scripts they're built on your poor narrator would have had to choose a whole different framework for hanging our tragicomedy on, but of course the narrative game-changer commonly known as the flick did serendipitously come along over there in "*La Ville-Lumiere*" (AKA Paris) so the silver screen and the classic director's chair and headwear and the Oscar and the Oscars after-party would one day have a reason for being and also so your narrator could take this perfect opportunity to say how about we FADE IN with respect to the following shot of the establishing persuasion: The exterior of a big economy motel at night. A large sign reading *Cinderella Inn* throws sickly neon all over the motel complex it names. Below the fantasy font of the *Cinderella* the sign features a happy likeness of the wretch/princess in question. She is still dressed in the rags she'll soon be zipping to the riches from as the story so famously goes. Presumably our dreamy-eyed diamond in the rough is reliving the night of her star-crossed and then suddenly uncrossed life.

In awful contrast a woman in the background starts breaking our hearts with her weeping.

It's a weeping hardly to be believed in its ability to make all within earshot and possibly even beyond not only re-feel every unnecessary bad thing that's ever happened to them and their entire ancestral line but also every bad thing that's ever happened to everybody else and their ancestors and every bad thing that will come to happen in the fullness of time in this setup if you will called existence in a cosmos that for some dumb unknown reason let the already-mentioned concept of faultiness weasel its way into it.

And yes, by "every bad thing" your narrator does mean to include this subjecting of you to such an inerasable weeping as this.

And now if you can, imagine that the weeping grows a bit distant and paradoxically stronger as the imaginary camera pulls back unlucky star-ward a little to take in the whole L-shaped, three-tiered stacking of one-and-a-half star guestrooms overlooking the parking lot of this motel in the middle of a certain crowning achievement of a certain crowning human achievement called a city and a civilization, respectively.

Of course, none of us can help wondering in which of the rooms the woman is killing us with her weeping.

THREE

And now with the help of a little cinematic magic here we all are crowded into the guestroom in question like a cloud of houseflies milling around on the dissonantly neutral blue walls.

A bare-naked man in his late twenties sits stunned at the foot end of the room's somewhat rumpled queen-size bed. A used condom droops lifelessly from his right hand.

This is FRANCIS, our hero. He is on the handsome side, with a build that is not quite to die for but is quite respectable nonetheless given his sedentary professional life and how little he does to keep himself up after working hours. When he meets people, our hero likes to say, "Hi, I'm Francis, like the Talking Mule." Among other things, this helps him foil the build-up of pressure that comes with taking himself too seriously or even seriously at all.

As we take in the male nudity, which in due time will prove to be mostly ungratuitous, we can't help noticing how at home Francis is in the sitting position and also how at home he is in taking it sitting down when he's visited for no good reason by a turn for the worse.

If you're dreading or hoping for a full-frontal shot, get over yourself. Just watch Francis listen to the weeping, which we now see is coming from behind the closed bathroom door. It is so terribly sad that it's all your narrator can do to keep subjecting us all to it.

If Francis, kind as he is, were to take over the narratorial duties while yours truly was getting a grip on himself, he'd say something like the following without moving his lips, or better yet, using the wonders of Voice Over: (In an Alabama half-wit's accent) "My mama always told me life is like a busted rubber." (In his own normal person voice) "Just kidding. Since my funny little baby brother died many years ago, my mom has said nothing remotely as colorful as all that. If you pressed her for some words of wisdom about what life is like, I think she would say it is like a sledgehammer. Or maybe a butcher knife. If you ask me, it is like a big flying monkey wrench with eyes on it."

Then yours truly, newly collected, would direct your attention to the old timey turntable on the room's west-most bedside chest. The record on it goes soundlessly round and round at 33 point 33 revolutions per minute or an even 2,000 revolutions per hour if you round up just a tiny bit (point two to be exact). As per what happens in a universe that has let defectiveness get its big fat foot in the door, the slick mechanism for returning the arm to the beginning is broken, so the needle just keeps riding the inside of the vinyl.

In the flickering light of a dozen romantic candles, we see an empty bottle of sparkling cider in an ice bucket on a coffee table. We see a dozen red roses. We see a woman's full-length rayon nighty (it's baby blue) draped with a heartbreaking extra emptiness over the room's other bedside chest. So badly does it hurt to think of the poor woman in the bathroom weeping without anything to cover her mother nakedness with that we look desperately for and find the absence of the coverlet she must have grabbed in her rush from the bed.

We watch Francis sit watching the room's broken clock flash 12 over and over and over as the well-known forces of spontaneous synchronization marshal the flashing twelves into a complicated alignment with the twelve instances of flickering and with the revolutions of the vinyl, which themselves are being relentlessly synced with the turning wheels within the wheel of Francis's unfortunate fortune.

Your omniscient narrator happens to know that it would have done Francis a world or more of good to have been in a position to bury his handsome face in hands unsmuttied by the yuck of his coming to find himself punked once again by the Trickster Figure that's been yucking it up all over the place since the day the first butt of a practical joke came along to give it a sick reason for being.

But then again, in a typical Catch-22, had all the yucky gapeseed (onetime Britishism for gobsmacker) not left Francis's hands otherwise occupied, there'd have been no need to hide his face in them.

FOUR

Faster than a speeding bullet, faster even than the speed of light in a perfect vacuum (which, of course, is never quite perfect), your omniscient and also extra omnipotent narrator has just zipped you at the risk of whiplash a whole decade down the road to a crowded café on nothing other, as luck would have it, than the first of the four extra special poetry nights in a certain cruelest of all months (according to nothing other than a poet) commonly known as April, which, of course, unfolds as National Poetry Month in a certain extra special country once the month in question's been kicked off by an inexplicable nod (called April Fools' Day) to the unwearyable Trickster Figure mentioned in the last chapter posing as a movie scene.

A spotlight shines on an open microphone on a slightly raised stage.

Francis comes into sort of blurry view at first as he stumbles drunkenly to the mic. He is looking a lot worse for the wear of the ten years that have passed since the disaster at the *Cinderella Inn.* You can just tell that he's still fully involved in the process of processing it all.

When Francis manages to reach center stage he begins fumblingly adjusting the microphone stand, ultimately shortening it to its lowest height. He taps the mic three times with a finger. It works. Francis bends over so his mouth is at mic level.

> FRANCIS (slurringly): Hi. I'm Francis, like the Talking Mule.

A wag in the crowd hee-haws.

> FRANCIS: Good one. Can't wait to hear your poem when it's your turn. Anyway, I've got a little poem here for y'all. Well actually, it's a poem plus a performance art piece within a poem. Is that going to

be ok? I don't think it quite violates the one-poem per person policy.

Francis looks offstage, gets the OK from the café's poetry night coordinator.

FRANCIS: Great. The piece is titled "Fucked in the Ass by the Star-Crossed Prophylactadon".

Francis clears his throat.

FRANCIS: Fucked in the Ass by the Star-Crossed Prophylactadon.

Francis assumes a very poetic demeanor.

FRANCIS: God tosses one icy clot of hard luck. Levels all his terrible lizards, who spend, oh, only about 65 thousand millenniums pooling the essence of their incredible collective penchant for being royally screwed in one fell swoop. Brewing, brewing, brewing in a soup of gooey crude oil in its greatest role as a broken prophylactic waiting untold eons to happen. Waiting, waiting, waiting. Dying, dying, dying to rise once more so it can go bust all over again and then, Eureka, up this unlucky muck is sucked through the human straw and is brought to the processing plant and then off it goes to the prophylactic factory, which spits out this little one and a half inch by one and a half inch package of cold-blooded petroleum-based doom—brings to pass the second coming of the star-crossed prophylactadon that springs from its flat and kinda crinkly little Pandora's Box and figuratively speaking proceeds to fuck me all Jurassically in the ass before dying a gooey death in my hand.

Our bard pantomimes his being anally raped by a terrible lizard, his face banging against the microphone with each cold-blooded thrust. He suspends the dramatization.

FRANCIS: No petroleum jelly.

He goes back to being face-bangingly sodomized, then stops.

FRANCIS: No sweet nothings.

More nonconsensual public sodomy. Another pause.

FRANCIS: Definitely no reach-around.

Even more sodomy. One more pause.

FRANCIS: Just...a good...hard...unlucky...fucking in the ass.

Over the ongoing amplified banging of Francis's face against the open mic as the thrusts quicken with the rapist's inching its way into big O territory, your omnipunctilious narrator would like to take it upon himself without delay to set the record straight by saying that even if that deposit of highly concentrated itch to take a royal screwing in one fell swoop out on our hero had originated in the Jurassic period like Francis's poem says it did, it would have been brewing and brewing and brewing and waiting and waiting and waiting and dying and dying and dying for one more thousand millenniums than the poem leads us to believe it was.

But, of course, as per the first chapter of the pretty definitive book you're holding in your very hands as we speak (unless, I guess, you're lucky enough to have someone in your life who is reading it to you while you're doing something else like, I don't know, recovering from a stroke or a fiery car or train wreck or a slip in the bathtub or something), it was all the way back on the far end (from this point of view) of the Triassic period that our story began in Pangea with that lounge of terrible lizards that gave their life to maintaining the family line only for it to be stopped on a dime thanks to that "icy clot of hard luck" that got itself tossed Earthward sometime before 66 million years ago.

FIVE

And now here we are on a city sidewalk in the middle of a Wednesday if memory serves, which, of course, it omnisciently does.

In white face paint and white gloves a mime tries undoing his confinement in an invisible box. He's attracted a modest crowd, at whose feet an upended beret waits for loose change and maybe a bill or two if this invisible box-incarcerated mime is lucky.

If you haven't guessed yet, the mime is none other than Francis. We are in the place we landed together upon instantly retracing our recent ten-year leap from the faulty rubber episode to the open mic night. If you're feeling a little like a boomerang, just go with that whole "no worries" outlook on life that comes in so handy when stuff to worry about pops up.

As we will soon find out, the earnings from this street performance are earmarked for the purchase of a certain rubber booby trap that a certain hopeless booby will go on shortly to insert his penis in. Do not read too much into that "shortly". Francis, if nothing else, was endowed down there with plenty for his purposes, which, it must be admitted, are pretty modest.

Anyway, to build a little on the dread of what we already know is coming while also at one and the same time and kind of paradoxically boosting my narrative credibility by demonstrating that I'm not so biased against life that I can't help showing it in only the very worst light, allow me to say this: If life were half a fraction crueler, we would right now be watching Francis bankroll his procurement of that "package of cold-blooded petroleum-based doom" by making squeaky balloon wiener dogs at some little brat's birthday party.

As we keep watching Francis flat-handedly keep feigning his

incarceration, go ahead and let your mind run wild with all he is wordlessly saying about what it means to be human.

And now even better than that let's imagine that Francis has been temporarily endowed with the powers of Voice Over for employing in our ears from a vantage point after our story is over.

> IMAGINARY FRANCIS (V.O.): It's hard to watch. I hate like heck to second guess a street-smart guy like myself, but in hindsight maybe I never should have ventured outside of my invisible little casing there. Maybe I should have just kept practicing the safest possible intercourse with the world.

Francis expertly mimes his escape through a tiny window in his invisible casing. He begins fruitlessly bending his steps into the gale-force headwind whose howling he secretly simulates without his mouth giving him away.

> IMAGINARY FRANCIS (V.O.): Can you hear that violent wind howling at me? It's saying, "Where do you think you're going, Bubble Boy? What on earth makes you think that after all these stormy years the world's got something nice in store for you at the end of that rainbow you're chasing?"

Angle on all the coins that have accumulated in the beret.

> IMAGINARY FRANCIS (V.O.): That right there is the hard cash that brought so much awful heartache.

Angle on Francis, who's now fully engaged in a life or death tug of war with some foe.

> IMAGINARY FRANCIS (V.O.): In the first draft of that poem you just heard, I traced the origin of those coins all the way back to the Big Bang. I can't tell you how hard it was to give up that pun in the second draft. Big Bang. Get it? At choice moments as I recited the poem I was going to inflate a condom a little bit more and a little bit more. And then at the

end, at the climactic mention of the popping of my bubble that was 14 billion years in the making [narrator's note: it was 13.8 billion years], I was going to pop the condom with a safety pin.

All Francis's herculean efforts in this tug of war are suddenly rewarded by a waggish letting go of the rope on the part of his foe, a prank that realistically sends Francis tumbling ass over teakettle backwards.

When his embarrassing momentum is spent, Francis mugs the shaking of a fist at his invisible opponent.

IMAGINARY FRANCIS (V.O.): Of course, I was going to title the poem "The Big Bang Heard Round My World".

Six

And now after a teeny tiny baby step time-wise, here we are in a drugstore on the same afternoon of the same Wednesday we just left. Francis stands in line at the check-out counter, a box of condoms in his hand.

Before forging ahead, let me mention that I thought Francis's imaginary Voice Over in that last chapter was spot on, if I do say so myself, which I do. I'm pretty omnisciently sure that you'll totally agree with me down the road of our story when your 20/20 or 20/15 or even 20/10 hindsight gives you a bird's eye view of how right a third-person narrator can be when he puts his mind to it. Or she. Or they. Or it. Or ze or hir or hen et alii et et cetera.

Getting back to the real Francis as he buys supplies for his ill-fated rainbow-chasing expedition as he himself just imaginarily characterized it, he's now next in line at the check-out counter.

Next to Francis stands a man of about Francis's age, height, and build. He is also exactly an eight and a half on the standard male beauty scale of the day, or would be if he weren't missing his entire left arm. Even your extra omniscient narrator is experiencing a little difficulty in nailing down precisely how many male beauty points and maybe fractions thereof were lost with the loss of the arm.

Anyway, this companion of Francis is named TONY. We will get to know him much better a little later. For now let's just glean some things about him based on the following exchange.

> TONY: She's not ready, Francis.
>
> FRANCIS: Yes she is, Tony.
>
> TONY: No she's not. She's not ready.
>
> FRANCIS: Is too.

TONY: Is not.

Francis withholds his rejoinder, lets the air clear for a minute.

FRANCIS: So, Tony. You're breaking into the rubber business. What name do you give your new brand?

Tony thinks about it for a moment.

TONY: Well. I suppose you could call it "Members Only".

Francis smiles, nods his appreciation.

TONY: She's not ready, Francis.

It is Francis's turn at the register, up to which he and Tony walk together like some kind of married couple.

FRANCIS (to the clerk): Young man, are these the very largest condoms you have?

Tony rolls his eyes at the clerk.

CLERK: I'm pretty sure.

The clerk rings up the condoms. Francis hands over the coins.

FRANCIS: I think I'm going to need to purchase one of your shoehorns then. What aisle can I find them on?

The clerk and Tony smile despite themselves. Francis smiles too. A big smudge of white face paint is still left from his recent street performance. Tony wipes it off for him.

It hurts, doesn't it, to see how ripe our poor hero was for being leveled by the big clot of hard luck that's so soon to come.

We follow Francis and Tony out of the store and onto the sidewalk. They become wrapped up in an animated conversation as they walk. We can't hear what they're saying, but we think we know the gist of it.

If Francis were to briefly reprise his role as the source of an imaginary Voice Over I believe that from his position here in the real time we're all inhabiting together right now he would say something to us along the lines of this: "I'll bet you're dying to know more about who that one-armed know-it-all is. I guess you'd have to call him my life partner—though he's been dead for a while now, two weeks and three days give or take a few to be exact."

We take a teeny tiny backward baby step to the scene where Francis is trapped in the invisible box. Angle on Tony, who steps out of the modest crowd to go up and drop some coins into the beret as a way to get the payments for services rendered started.

We now take a giant leap to a certain first open mic poetry night in a certain cruel month commonly known as April. Francis's face bangs into the microphone. Angle on Tony, who sits at a table looking even worse than Francis for the wear of the ten years between the pantomime scene and this one.

> IMAGINARY FRANCIS (V.O.): We weren't a gay couple or anything. At least I don't think we were.

Francis's banging stops. After a pause, the crowd politely claps. Tony, as drunk as Francis or more, makes the sound of one hand wildly clapping. It's quite heart-wrenching knowing what I know.

> IMAGINARY FRANCIS (V.O.): How to explain Tony? I know, let's do a quick video biography. What do you say?

SEVEN

SCHOOL ROOM - DAYTIME

A sixth-grade boy sits at his desk staring at a blank sheet of paper, a pencil poised in his one remaining hand. The boy's classmates sit at their respective desks madly writing away.

The boy, if you haven't guessed yet, is our hero's life partner Tony, who of course is a more than worthy focus of our attention in his own right. It's his first day back after having his left arm ripped off. Looks like he might be experiencing a little touch of writer's block. He's supposed to be cranking out a 500-word essay on what he thinks ancient Greece's greatest contribution to humanity was.

Bummer that Tony can't hold a pencil and ruminatingly rub his chin or scratch his head at the same time like the other kids can do to get the juices in their twelve-year-old brains flowing in something other than the usual pre- or full-blown pubescent directions.

You're probably saying to yourself, "Well, at least it wasn't the right arm that Tony had ripped from him." Nice try, but Tony, of course, was one of the only one in seven and a half of us who are left-handed (even after factoring in the one in a hundred of us who are half left-handed thanks to the wonders of ambidextrousness). Here, let me show you what Tony was happy-go-luckily doing with himself just before he got mistaken for some kind of overgrown divine child's Mr. Potatohead whose whole left arm you can just yank off anytime you want to.

CUT TO: TWO-LANE HIGHWAY – DAYTIME

Twelve-year-old Tony sits behind the driver's seat in his family economy car. His dad drives. His mom sits in the passenger seat next to the dad. All are in their Sunday bests as they barrel north toward the Catholic mass they're running a little late for as luck, or rather its exact opposite, would have it. A plastic Jesus serenely rides the dashboard, believe it or not. Keep this detail in mind for later.

In the southbound lane the cars periodically whiz by without incident as per the astronomical odds against what's about to happen.

Tony's window is down. His left arm is extended out wing-like into all the onrushing windless Sunday morning air. With the littlest hint of dramatic foreshadowing, Tony's sort of disembodied arm lazily rides the car-generated wind up and down and up and down as he shifts the flattened hand giving his arm over to the universe's newish forces of human-powered flight. On his wrist out there Tony wears a nice watch. Yeah yeah. Tony knows it's supposed to go on the off hand.

Anyway, the above is what Tony was up to just before a big literal monkey wrench fell out of the bed of an oncoming service truck and tossed a big figurative kind of monkey wrench in Tony's flight plans. That watch you're looking at out there is brand new. Tony got it for his birthday. In just a minute or so, a northbound car will run over it, along with the arm it's attached to.

Angle on Tony's face.

He's whaling out all of "Stairway to Heaven" in his head so as not to subject his parents to "that jungle music" as they call it. By this point in his young life Tony has already become a quite accomplished air guitarist. The reason his prized watch is not on his off hand is that he loves the flash it adds when he's windmilling away at his imaginary axe in the manner of Pete Townsend if he were left-handed.

What Tony is soon going to find out is that a lot of the fun goes out of whaling on a pretend guitar if you have to do it with a pretend arm. Ever seen a speeding ton of irony— actually, it's more like two tons.

CUT TO: SERVICE TRUCK

18

As the truck speeds along, a big monkey wrench nefariously inches its way thanks to a set of worn out shock absorbers toward the edge of the open bed.

Angle on the driver's door, which features the company name and logo. The name is Ganesh Fix-It. The logo is a dancing bipedal elephant with a tool in the hand of each of its four arms.

Swear to god, Tony lost his main arm to a big monkey wrench belonging to a fix-it company named after a big, many-armed Hindu figure in charge of giving us all a hand in life. You can't make this shit up.

Angle on the big peripatetic monkey wrench. (We conveniently can't help noticing that "Ganesh Fix-It" has been stamped on the handle. This information will come in handy in some chapters to come when the close readers among you start wondering how grown-up Francis and Tony are keeping the wolf from their door.)

Angle on the sky. See that right there. That is the heaven that Led Zeppelin was talking about. That is where the inspiration for that plastic figurine on Tony's family dashboard comes from.

Up there is where not one single finger is being lifted to keep that monkey wrench on the flatbed for just the extra teeny tiniest of an infinitely splittable second it would have taken for Tony's life arc to probably have included the making of a name for himself at the inaugural Air Guitar World Championships that would be held in Oulu, Finland in a mere handful of summers (a right handful for Tony) after the world lost what might well have been its premier air guitar prodigy.

And by "one single finger", of course, I mean a certain very first first finger that transferred life itself like it was a bolt of static electricity on a dry, cold day into the whole universe's second first finger, the one planted there, as a certain storied overhead visual story goes, on the left hand of a certain star-crossed, progeny-damning father of humanity that the star-crossed Jesus was said to be the Second Adam in relation to.

And of course the above is not even to mention how perfectly everything had to have been busy falling into place since the beginning of spacetime for the parabolic arc of a three-pound clot of hard luck posing as a metaphorically pregnant chunk of ductile iron bouncing off a long-awaiting point of perfectly climate-primed tarmac to dead end at exactly the juncture where existence delivered the one and only point on a twelve-year-old boy where a projectile with exactly the right mass and exactly the right hardness on the Vickers and every other scale and exactly the right angular and other kinds of momentum could have severed the left arm clean as a whistle. (And of course by iron I mean that very last elemental contribution to the universe that the star-crossed stars cough up in the throes of their inevitable violent deaths.)

And of course the paragraph above is also not to mention how impossibly hard it was for poor Tony's star-crossed father to understand why the hands the Lord's got the whole world in as the story goes couldn't have hustled his son's mother through her grooming routine in preparation for church enough for the family car to have crossed paths with the Ganesh Fix-It truck before the monkey wrench fell off it without the hands in question or any of the fingers on them doing anything, as mentioned, to reward the boy's loving father for his countless months of Sundays'-worth of devoted church-going.

EIGHT

Just so you know, this break in the middle of our quick video biography of Tony was meant to provide a moment for the last chapter to sink in while also offering the dear reader a natural chance to go give a loved one a big hug with the two arms that most of us are lucky enough to hold onto till the very end for all the other stuff we've probably lost.

And now back to the show. More specifically, here we are in the classroom where we last saw Tony beating his head against a case of writer's block. But now Tony's seat is empty. A sheet of paper sits blankly still on the desktop. All around the empty seat, Tony's classmates still pitch into singing the praises of ancient Greece.

If the scene were being graced by a Voice Over from our imaginary Francis, it would go something like this: "Hey everybody, where'd Tony go?"

CUT TO: SCHOOL HALLWAY

Tony walks briskly, the oversized hall pass tucked under his arm so he can squeeze his penis with the one hand he has left for doing so. Out the back side of his Robert Plant bellbottoms the untied laces of the shoe on his left (as opposed to our right as he walks briskly but also gingerly toward us) are dragging their aglets. Yes folks, Tony knows his shoelace is dangerously untied. He knows all about the face plant that's coming if he trips while the one hand he has left for breaking a fall is otherwise occupied with keeping himself from pissing himself. What's he supposed to do about it?

CUT TO: BOYS ROOM

Tony stands dancing at a urinal as he struggles with his stuck zipper. The quarter-inch plywood hall pass clatters to the floor. It is a likeness of Socrates, the star-crossed Father of Western Philosophy, who for his part famously never had to deal with the diuretic consequences of his last beverage ever.

He has landed face-up, so we can see that etched into the bottom of this gift-shop chachki is this bit of his wisdom: "There is no solution, seek it lovingly."

Pretty unlovingly Tony is wishing ill against the whole zipper apparatus that is solutionlessly stuck on the exception it is taking to unclenching its teeth without the usual one hand holding onto the top of the fly while the other is manning the pull tab on the slider, which is also known as the car for all you readers out there with extra inquiring minds.

It's almost like on top of everything else, Tony's undergoing a touch of performance anxiety as he dances in the little boys room in full creepy view of us and also Socrates who for all intents and purposes is watching him not un-Socratically calling into question the severe minimalist's message to us all in the famous question of his that goes, "How many things can I do without?"

Now that not just one but two pearls of Socrates's wisdom have shown up in this one bathroom scene, I might as well say as a side note that the following string of other pearls attributed to that impious and capitally punished corrupter of young men would also serendipitously have lent the chapters to come a ton of retrospective thematic resonance: "Be kind, for everyone you meet is fighting a hard battle"; "He [and she] is richest who is content with the least"; "Beware of the barrenness of a busy life".

Anyway, getting back to Tony, he's still bathroom-dancing his ass off as he does without the hand his fly's so adamantly demanding. Look at him go. This is only 1981. Believe it or not, River Dancing is still a good decade away from capturing the imagination of the world. Imagine me whistling a breakneck Irish ditty.

Finally, Tony gets his bellbottoms dropped so he can take a baby hop the rest of the way to the urinal and relieve his bladder while we watch him from behind.

Here's an interesting side note. Tony lost his arm in the very same week he learned to jerk off. Only one time in his whole life did he ever get to pleasure himself with his favorite hand. At no time was he ever able tenderly to cup his nuts with one hand while working himself over with the other—one of the great pleasures in the autoerotic life of the male of our species.

CUT TO: SCHOOL HALLWAY

Tony earnestly heads to the boys room. He's wearing different clothes than what we've seen him in. For one thing, he's wearing sweatpants. This, obviously, is a whole new day relative to the one we just left.

CUT TO: SCHOOL HALLWAY

Tony steps lively down the now familiar hallway in responding once again to the call of nature in her greatest role as a stuck record (go ahead and let this choice of metaphor zoom you forward for a moment to that earlier motel room scene) where Tony's concerned.

CUT TO: SCHOOL HALLWAY

Tony's responding once again to Nature's call. He enters the boys room. The door closes behind him. We focus on the BOYS sign.

The reason Tony keeps having to go to the little boys room is that he has developed Type 1 diabetes.

CUT TO: BOYS ROOM

Tony stands with his back to us again at the urinal.

That's syrup he's pissing. You could pour it over a stack of pancakes.

CUT TO: HIGHWAY – DAY

Tony's dad—remember him?—drives the family car all alone down the road. He looks extremely sad. The plastic Jesus no longer rides the dashboard.

This is the highly probable source of Tony's diabetes. A little while back relative to the timeframe of the boys room montage, he caught a virus likely thanks to his sadness-stripped immune system and or to all the times he took the Lord's name in vain after that ill-fated Sunday when the family never quite made it to church.

This virus Tony's own dad gave to Tony. The dad made a full recovery. The son did too, except that his pancreas had been cooked. At least that's what the doctors think.

CUT TO: BOYS ROOM

Tony struggles to zip up his bellbottoms.

We're back to Tony's first day at school after losing his arm. Now he is simply trying to zip up the hip huggers he was just struggling to unzip. Let's say you can literally hear the clock ticking on the 500-word essay assignment waiting for him back in the classroom.

Tony gives up a moment, then stiffens his upper lip and goes back to struggling with the zipper. If he weren't in a boys room with his pants undone, we'd all want to give him a big group hug. At least your narrator would.

Going back to the diabetes thing, while I suppose young Tony bears some responsibility for the sheering off of the arm he did stick out the window of a fast-moving vehicle on a two-lane highway after all, what was he supposed to do about his pancreas? I mean, it's known as the "hidden organ" for god's sake. He couldn't have found it even if he'd wanted to expose it to the slings and arrows and big-ass flying monkey wrenches of outrageous fortune. And still a big flying metaphysical monkey wrench comes along and in one fell swoop converts sugar into Tony's mortal enemy for life.

CUT TO: CLASSROOM

Tony sort of fists his way left-handedly, as we're known to say here in this right-hand-centric world, through his essay.

He's on his new version of a roll. Inspired by his recent Sisyphean labors in the boys room, he is gushing if you will about what a great and convenient invention the toga was, especially at parties serving alcoholic beverages, which are well known to make you have to go pee, and so on. Amazingly, Tony finds 501 words of praise for the toga, almost half of which can actually be read.

Angle on the teacher, a man, whose sadness shows as he sits at his desk watching Tony learn how to write all over again.

Under the circumstances, the teacher will find it in his heart to overlook Tony's abominable penmanship. He will have to mark Tony down a little bit for content, though, in light of the toga's being a Roman and not a Greek contribution to the world.

Angle on a kid in the back row of seats. That's young Francis pouring himself right-handedly into the task at hand. I know a lot of yakety-yaking has been going on for a cinematic format like this, so how about we zoom in for a little semi-gratuitous nudity?

We move to a close-up of Francis's handiwork, which he now sits admiring. He has been drawing a picture of the armless Venus de Milo. The bare breasts are incredibly voluptuous.

Va va voom, eh? Look at that picture stand there saying a thousand words—all in a husky irresistible whisper. Those are possibly the best breasts Francis had ever drawn up to that point. Francis, you should know, loves breasts. I know. Everybody loves breast, especially perfect ones. But Francis really really, and I mean really really, loves them. Remember that. It becomes important much later.

Anyway, to give you a sense of just how memorably Francis nailed this essay assignment, let me assure you that to this day if you asked him about it he would remember and even feel in his bones if you will the raging boner he gave himself with that 1000-word visual essay on the Greeks' greatest gift to the world.

We watch Francis fuss a minute with the last touches on the

left breast from his and our perspective.

At first, Francis titled his essay, "I love you this much", but it occurred to him just in the nick of time that this otherwise perfect title might give the teacher the wrong idea in a number of ways. So, Francis titled it, "Look Ma, No Arms". In a dialogue bubble coming from her pretty mouth, he had Venus de Milo herself apologize to the teacher for him going over the 500-word limit with this 1000-word picture. She asked him to pretty please just give Francis extra credit for the 500 extra words plus the four words in the title for a total of 504 extra credit points.

The teacher will turn down Venus de Milo, the naked, handicapped goddess of love herself. In fact, Francis will get no credit for his efforts at all. On the bright side, he will have no trouble at all contenting himself with the thought that at least he probably gave his teacher a smile, and maybe a boner.

On the other hand, Francis will kick himself for the academic ambitiousness that blinded him to the right move of having Venus ask the teacher to give Tony however many of his extra credit words it took to bring his friend up to the 500 legible word mark.

Angle on all the sixth graders hammering away at their essays.

Look at 'em all go. Democracy. Geometry. Modern medicine. Human drama in three acts. Columns of all shapes and sizes. The Archimedean Screw. Bare naked Olympic wrestling. The word "callipygian", which of course refers to well-formed buttocks. Ok, maybe not that last one or two. But, you know what I mean. A bunch of 11 and 12-year-olds wrapping their little brains around big, grand, all-important things. I can say with no shadow of a doubt in my extra omniscient mind that had Francis known then what Francis knows now, his picture would have been of some Grecian guy looking agape into the eyes of the utterly discomforted viewer. The title would have been, "Agape", the Greek word for god's love of humankind and for humankind's unselfish love for one another. The picture would have spoken a thousand words about how at the heart of humankind's side of divine agape is a standing agape with disbelief at how god could let all our poor brothers and sisters suffer so much pain.

NINE

Here we are in what can only be a school detention room. Or possibly the early adolescent boy section of a makeshift shelter during a natural disaster like an earthquake or a hurricane and or flood or a wildfire or a virus outbreak or a comet-strike or even an unnatural disaster like a war or uprising or some kind of man and woman or machine learner-made apocalypse or something.

As per usual, our first impression, though, was the correct one.

Francis and Tony sit across from one another at one of the room's long tables. Next to them, two similarly arranged boys take turns flicking a little triangularly folded piece of paper in its greatest role as a football through the goalposts their partner simulates with his two index fingers and two thumbs. Tony watches from his increasingly familiar spot on the sidelines.

For his part, Francis sits threading a needle.

You probably thought that last chapter break meant we were finally done with Tony's backstory. I'm sorry to say we're not. I'm sorry partly because we are getting way behind in this first act of this human drama. The extra sensitive ears of your extra omniscient narrator can actually hear Aristotle, also known as "The Brain" thanks to Plato, keep saying *"viasteite"*, which of course means "hurry it up" in Greek, which you would know if you were also extra omniscient.

Anyway, Francis and Tony are in detention because the former got caught red-handedly injecting the latter's insulin for him again even though both have been told a thousand times that only the school nurse is allowed to do it.

The needle threaded, Francis begins sewing up an all but buttonless polo shirt whose long left sleeve he has torn off using his teeth before this scene began. He is doing this to

Tony's brand new shirt because, of course, Tony can't do it and also because the job of cutting off and sewing up the left sleeves of her son's new shirts just makes Tony's poor mom way too brutally sad.

Angle on one of the other delinquents. He has pushed his seat way way back from the table. He holds up his goalpost. The suspense builds a little as we tell ourselves there's no way the boy's partner is going to try this impossibly long field goal, the equivalent of a then unprecedented 64-yarder in non-imaginary spacetime and with a non-imaginary football and foot for kicking it. His partner tries the impossibly long field goal.

It's…it's…it's…good!

Angle on Tony, who's quite happy for his fellow bad apple. Every fiber of his being wants to make the super exuberant and not un-involuntary universal sign of the football score. If he tried to heed the fibers of his being's urgings, though, the already skeptical detention room duty would think Tony was asking to go to the bathroom again.

In the background, we hear Francis blurt, "Shit." Angle on the stink eye from the detention room duty. Reverse angle on Francis, who has just pricked his finger with the sewing needle. Francis is squeezing the finger, his inherited version of the earlier-mentioned first one on the left hand of Adam's descendants, drawing a bead of blood.

At the risk of frittering away a bit of my omnimeticulously built-up credibility as a narrator you can count on, let's CUT directly on the nose TO:

A BATHROOM STALL

where Tony sits on the toilet seat and Francis pricks his finger, drawing a bead of blood. Tony watches as Francis tests the spot of blood he's collected on a testing strip.

It's weird that in only 43,125 more little prickings, Tony will be dead.

TEN

Here we are in a park on a school holiday, and sorry Aristotle, but no we're not quite done with Tony's backstory, so STFU.

We're here to watch Francis and Tony, in beautiful unison, do a jazzercise routine, each lipping the words to the same disco song in their heads. Feel free to plug in any disco song you like, and my apologies if it gets stuck in your head.

Anyway, this is the exercise regimen that Francis implemented when he read at the library how physical activity can help the body use insulin better. It's quite heartwarming but also a tiny bit bittersweet to know how many fewer little prickings Tony would have lived to rack up if the two bosom buddies hadn't religiously kept their jazzercising up over the years.

CUT TO: SCHOOL GYM

The sixth-grade P.E. class is square dancing. In his eightsome, Tony promenades with his partner, who holds Tony's right hand and pretty unconvincingly pretends to hold his left.

You can tell Tony is freaking the living bejesus out of this really cute blue-eyed and dark-haired girl he's sweet on. He's still particularly smitten by the way she smiled at him that one time before he lost his arm.

There she is all weirded out by the phantom hand she's holding, and you know what Tony's all self-conscious about? All Tony can think about in this scene is the pimple on the end of his nose.

Angle on Tony's self-consciousness, with the pimple on his nose blurred out, out of respect for him. As it so happens, the blemish in question was a harbinger of the outbreak of acne that plagued Tony day in and day out without letup for the next three years he spent somewhere between a four and a low five on the male beauty scale.

It will be like a thousand-day game of facial whack-a-mole where the labour of moles as they're collectively known don't go back to where they came from without a messy fight. You can also call it a "company" of moles, which is probably even more apropos when you think about what constant companions these curses were to poor Tony.

At this point in our story Tony is still too proud to ask Francis for help with this pimple that evilly has resisted all Tony's one-handed attempts to pop it.

We pull away from the focus on Tony, take in all the eightsomes being put through their paces by the square dance caller, a feller in a cheesy, easily pictured cowboy outfit. Feel free to make the connection between this cow and sixth-grader poking son of a gun and whatever heartless manner of cosmic-grade control freak it is that's been putting all of creation through its paces since the jump.

I am not going to show you Tony during his three-year acne scourge. It would make you think less of him. You know it would. Even though it wasn't his fault at all. He did everything he could. He did the constant washing in gentle circles. He did the drying in gentle dabs. He applied the right chemicals. He got the sleep and steered clear of the chocolate and the greasy foods and did everything else that Francis's research at the library told him he should do.

Ok fine, he did masturbate, but Jesus Christ, wouldn't you jerk yourself off now and then for comfort if it was becoming increasingly clear that you were going to be the one and only lover you would ever have?

ELEVEN

Twelve-year-old Francis and Tony sit peacefully together on a park bench as if they, like us (up to and including Aristotle), are happy that Tony's sad video backstory is finally over.

For a moment, in the middle of all the busy processing of our ever-thickening plot, we simply watch the two friends take a load off in their favorite spot. Ok. Downtime's over.

> FRANCIS: So Tony. What would you do if you could have your arm back for one hour?

> TONY: Well. I think I would go find a monkey and use my right arm to beat him over the head with my left arm for whatever part he played in the invention of the monkey wrench.

Francis smiles. That right there is one big reason Francis loved Tony so much.

> FRANCIS: No. I mean, if your left arm was attached again to your body.

Tony thinks this over.

> FRANCIS: I know what you would do. You would get a motel room and spend an hour spanking a different monkey.

This cracks Tony up. That's another big reason Francis loved Tony.

It is terrible to think that in not all that many years Tony will die in Francis's arms in that very spot.

Going back to that thing about a motel room and the merciless abusing of a monkey, isn't it something how even the simple day-to-day life of a hero in his younger years can give a narrator who's on the ball a subtle but totally golden opportunity to both foreshadow and come back to a key plot point like the one where Francis is ambushed at the

Cinderella Inn by the merciless forces in charge of making a monkey of the star-crossed ones among us who fall for the horseshit about love conquering all.

TWELVE

You're welcome for that short chapter number eleven. I'm of course well aware that modern-day life hasn't exactly been kind to the span of human attention on folks other than ourselves. Just so you know, this chapter's going to be a doozy. Hang in there if you can. If it helps, there's going to be wrestling and nudity.

To avert a distracting jag of déjà vu, I should probably trigger alert you to the news that we're in the narratorial limbo before my returning you to the daytime sidewalk scene where we last saw Francis and Tony having that animated conversation you might already have forgotten about in the hustle bustle of the personal corner of the modern-day world keeping you from reading our story straight through so you don't forget important details between readings.

It's the scene immediately following your heartbreakingly cocky hero talking about shoehorning his manhood into one of his new balloons. The faulty one, if you recall. In the original check-in with our hero and his friend at this point in our story, we all correctly assumed the two were still arguing about whether Robin was ready to have sex with Francis or not.

This time around, we follow the two young men as they walk, and while we're at it we're also following the back and forth between them as you'll very soon notice.

> TONY: Who are you going to listen to, Francis, your best friend or your penis?

> FRANCIS: You've been bugging me so much today, Tony, that my penis is now my best friend. Besides, it isn't my penis telling me to have sex with Robin. My penis inphallusably knows when to keep his own counsel, as opposed to a certain former best friend of mine, the one who's slipped to fourth place on my best friend list, right below my heart and my soul,

which are both telling me to listen to every fiber of my being telling me it's time to have sex with Robin before I've missed the perfect moment.

TONY: But she's not ready, Francis.

FRANCIS: You have now fallen below every fiber of my being on my best friend list, Tony. Hope you're happy way down there.

TONY: I'm not. Because every fiber of my being is telling me the moment isn't perfect yet.

To his credit, Francis does not point out to Tony that he (Francis) has more fibers of his being (because he's not missing an arm) and therefore would win a free and fair whole-body democratic vote on the matter.

To your narrator's slight chagrin, Francis also does not call Tony a stuck record at any point in this run-up to the horrible motel room scene, which of course would have been a golden opportunity to subtly look ahead to and at the same time look back on that memorable record stuck on evoking a ground zero spinning out the terrible mental loops that thanks to the wonders of the already mentioned spontaneous synchronization would go on for the next ten years to plague Francis at a rate of thirty-three and a third revolutions per minute.

Getting back to the present moment, Francis stops walking, holds the box of condoms out to Tony, who has also stopped.

FRANCIS: Could you hold these, please?

Tony takes the box like the good former best friend that he is. Francis very deliberately inserts the index finger of his left hand into his left ear and then inserts the index finger of his right hand into his right ear.

Francis then resumes walking and Tony follows like the good former best friend and also good loser that he is.

FRANCIS: La la la la la la la la.

Francis's acting like a big baby like this begins to make us wonder if he himself is ready for a grown-up undertaking like having sex with another person.

CUT TO: ART STUDIO DRESSING ROOM

> ART TEACHER: Francis. Your friend is missing an arm.

Francis looks at Tony, looks back at the art teacher, whose features you should feel free to fill in for yourselves.

> FRANCIS: It's not so much that it's missing. Really, it's more like it's gone for good.

> ART TEACHER: Francis. I told you. I need someone who can pose with you as a Greek wrestler.

> FRANCIS: The last time I was at a museum, it seemed pretty clear to me that the Greeks saw arms as totally optional. Besides, Tony is quite callipygianate. Greek artists loved that.

> ART TEACHER: Calli- what?

> FRANCIS: -pygianate. The Greek way to say a person's got a well-formed buttocks.

The art teacher looks at Tony, who makes a show of blushing.

> FRANCIS: Here's what we tell your students. We are staging the all-out showdown between the one and only winner of the regular, able-bodied Olympics, me, and one of the many many many many winners of the Special Olympics, where everyone is well known to be a winner.

> TONY: I pity the fool.

Francis smiles. The art teacher just shakes her or his head depending on what sex and or gender you gave him or her or them in your mind's eye.

CUT TO: ART STUDIO

Up on a slightly raised platform, Francis and Tony, naked and well-oiled, stand frozen in a wrestlers' clinch while a roomful of art students render them in charcoal. (We won't get into how thought-provoking it is that our story's two main animate beneficiaries of carbon's 13 billion-year-old existence are being brought to two-dimensional life many times over by little lifeless fistful's of charcoal.)

Anyway, there's the nudity I promised. Want to see their penises? Forget it. It wouldn't be fair to Francis, who's a grower and not a shower like Tony. You'd think less of our hero if you saw him being overshadowed manhood-wise. You know you would.

Angle on Tony's spectacular backside. See what I mean about Tony's buttocks?

We return to a relatively discreet sideshot of the grapplers. The following exchange takes place in whispers, with a minimum of lip movement.

>TONY: Robin's very fragile, Francis.

>FRANCIS: I know that, Tony. That's why it's so lucky that I'm so strong.

>TONY: You're not that strong.

>FRANCIS: Yes I am. Robin's love has brought out the inner Hercules in me. When I'm finished kicking your well-formed buttocks here, I think I'll go slay the Many-Headed Hydra just for fun.

>TONY: I really don't think you're as strong as you think you are, Francis.

>FRANCIS: I think I'm actually stronger than I think I am.

>TONY: I think that actually doesn't make any sense. How can you think you're stronger than you think you are?

>FRANCIS: That's a really good question, Socrates. I

think I'll wrestle with it as soon as I'm finished kicking about an Augean Stable's worth of shit out of you.

TONY: Francis. I mean, Hercules. How can I put this? Maybe you're a fighter and not a lover. I mean, sure, you're really good at throttling a snake—

FRANCIS: Really good. Been doing that since I was a baby.

TONY: Yeah. But how familiar are you with the art of being with someone other than yourself?

FRANCIS: Now that's a low blow. I wouldn't have expected that from a Special Olympian.

TONY: All I'm saying is, do you really want to make like the Cretan Bull and go charging right into the china shop of Robin's maidenhood?

FRANCIS: So you're calling me a cretin now?

TONY: Different Cretan.

FRANCIS: Oh.

Angle on one of the art students, who's about 750 words into his thousand-word picture of our hero and the worthy opponent he's locked horns with.

FRANCIS: I see your point. I do. I guess I am something of a greenhorn in the ways of our gal Aphrodite. Maybe I just need a little experience. Hey, I know. How about I practice a little on you, Spartacus? Mind if I jam my big fat Greek penis in your big fat Greek ass?

TONY: I thought you said I was callipygianate.

FRANCIS: I was lying.

Silence ensues.

FRANCIS: Come on, Spartacus. There's no pouting in bare naked Olympic wrestling.

TONY: I must look like a big fat greased pig up here.

FRANCIS: Come on, soldier. Chins up.

TONY: It's just that I love baklava so much.

FRANCIS: Don't beat up on yourself. That's not an Olympic event. There's no laurel wreath to be won in that.

TONY: Gee, Hercules. It's so kind of you to be seen in the ring with a big fat superheavyweight like me.

FRANCIS: Now, now. It's not only about leanness and muscle. Sometimes, I kinda wish my ass wasn't so chiseled. I mean, I'm sure you would have totally been Plato's pet. He would have been all over you, man.

TONY: You're just saying that.

FRANCIS: No I'm not.

TONY: Really?

Angle on Tony and Francis from the back of the room. If they're still chattering, we don't hear them and no movement of their lips is giving them away.

If this chapter, and this whole first act for that matter, weren't running so long, I'd show you Francis and Tony platonically helping each other get all the grease off their semi-hard bodies after this Olympic encounter—which they fought to a draw, by the way.

Such a wiping of each other off would have said retrospective volumes when we get to later chapters. I think I will take the time right now, though, to mention that you will come to know how poignant a sign of Francis's emotional resourcefulness it was for him to make light of Plato's unplatonic preying on the boys.

THIRTEEN

Here we are at a park on a nice afternoon. By now, you should recognize this as Francis and Tony's favorite spot, particularly since the two young men are sitting right there on their bench.

I should show you why Tony was such a doubting Thomas about how strong Francis thought he was in the days leading up to his rushing like a Cretan Bull into the china shop of Robin's maidenhood. We're going to have to do our best to make Francis's backstory shorter than Tony's, though, since Act 1 really should be just about over.

CUT TO: FRANCIS'S CHILDHOOD HOUSE

A chubby little two-year-old boy in only a diaper stands in the middle of the living room aping an orangutan. His eyes shine like no others. One of his hands waggles overhead. With the other he waves a banana. If we didn't know better, we'd swear the young little chunkster is pulling off a decent swing dance.

What you're looking at is hands-down the biggest goofball the universe has ever poured all its raw materials and all its physical laws and all the metaphysical cards up its sleeve and other stuff into producing. His name is Lewis. He thinks he's King Louis, the King of the Swingers, AKA the Jungle VIP, from the *Jungle Book*, Lewis's favorite movie by a mile judging by the thousand or so times he has watched the Mowgli story end to end by this time in his short life.

In reality, this is Francis's kid sibling. Francis was seven when his oops baby brother came along. Up to then, Francis had been so madly racing his ass off through the Piaget stages on his way to the adult life of an A-type that in his back pocket he had all the drive and all the competitive spirit and organizational skills and the perfectionism needed to keep his A+ type dad more or less proud of him for stuff like situating himself at the head of his class for three years running.

Angle on nine-year-old Francis sitting on a couch taking great lazy pleasure in his little brother's antics.

We watch King Louis stick the banana halfway down the front of his diaper. The other half of the banana sticks out suggestively as the Jungle VIP struts around like simian royalty. Your narrator's and his dear readers' fixation on the penis couldn't hold a candle to Francis's baby brother's.

LEWIS: Ooo ooo ooo, ee ee, oo oo ee oo oo.

No, that is not Lewis masterfully matching the classic sounds that a monkey makes. That is him trying to say "Oh, oobee doo, I wanna be like you oo oo." The truth is that Lewis is way behind with respect to all the well-known developmental mileposts except those associated with old-timey dancing and fooling around. The more loving but firm nudges he's gotten from mom and dad, the further he's fallen behind.

It is his big brother Francis, accomplished as he is already at concrete operational thought, who does Lewis an immeasurable solid by bringing all his precocious powers of reasoning to bear, so to speak, on convincing the mom and the dad that it's Baloo's and not Lewis's fault that his human progress is a little on the slowgoing side as he makes his lazy way to the day that his eye is caught by something beautiful that the rat race has to offer.

Going back to that thing about the tough-love nudges and Lewis's equal and opposite reaction to them, it's not unreasonable at all for the dear reader right now, even though we ourselves are getting behind relative to the pace our story's supposed to be proceeding at, to use her or his own longstanding powers of reason to entertain the idea that whether he knows it or not, little two-year-old Lewis is making a highly elaborate mockery of the Promethean bee in our bonnet at the heart of our species' Darwinianly separating ourselves from the likes of the tree swingers whose king sings lines like, "I've reached the top and had to stop and that's what's bothering me," and lines like, "What I desire is man's red fire," and like, "Give me the power of man's red flower so I can be like you."

Recall if you will that the camera has been pointing at nine-year-old Francis lounging on a couch. Let's let the imaginary version of the man he grew up to be do the Voice Over honors.

> IMAGINARY MAN FRANCIS (V.O.): We monkeyed around like this together pretty much every day, pretty much all day long when it wasn't a school day for me. In a minute, Lewis will bop on over and grab my hand and make me get up and do the jazzy Baloo dance around the house with him while I sing "The Bare Necessities" over and over again like a good kind of stuck record. If my little brother had lived we'd likely have forgotten all about our worries and our strife like this all the way till 1994 when the remake of *The Jungle Book* came out to reinforce our carefree way of life in eerily the same year that *The Lion King* came along to second Baloo's unforgettable message by featuring Timon and Pumbaa singing "Hakuna Matata" to a certain once-fun-loving little lion cub up to his ears in worries and strife.

CUT TO: DINING ROOM – EVENING

Six-year-old Francis sits eating at the dinner table with the mom and dad he's the only child of at this point in the arc of their star-crossed family life. Francis's fork-and-knife-work, of course, is outstanding, miles ahead of the curve. His posture is just about perfect. The vegetables on his plate are well on their way to being eaten down to the last one. To his mom's great but understated pleasure, her son's hair is still as perfectly self-parted as it was when the day started. The red fire of the A-type-in-training is visibly blossoming there in our hero's eyes.

Angle on the go-getting old block Francis is the chip off of.

42

The full-blown red fire in his eyes makes it hard if not impossible to see the gleam that will soon turn into Lewis.

If the screwball B-minus-type that Francis went on to become were doing the Voice Over right now, he'd say, "Up to this point, I think the last time anybody in our family line had had a good laugh was when actual monkeys were swinging in our family tree, flinging dookie at one another and playing with their bananas to beat the band."

CUT TO: DINING ROOM

Eight-year-old Francis sits eating again at the dinner table with his mom and dad. We can't help noticing that his posture isn't quite as close to perfect as it once was. There is something much different about the fire in his eyes. It's somehow more orange now than red. Kind of a vivid tangelo or a goldfish or a Crayola or mimosa or even a plain old pumpkin orange.

Angle, of course, on one-year-old Lewis sitting in his highchair at one head of the table with his onesie all the way off. He has grown from the gleam his and his big brother's father and mother didn't even know the onetime head of the household had in his eye into a tub of happy baby fat threatening to leave him stuck a la Winnie the Pooh in his mealtime highchair.

The new bare-chested head of the Francis family household is covered head-to-toe in his dinner. It is ridiculously easy to see how this large dollop of human cottage cheese grew up to be the lotus-eating swing dancer from two scenes ago. Lewis quite delightedly flings a fistful of something mushy at his big brother. He would hurl a load of good-natured baby trash talk at him too if he weren't so far behind the verbal learning curve.

Angle on Francis, his mom and his dad. All are roughly the same kind and amount of tickled by the baby's monkey business.

Lewis, with a goofy repeated craning of his neck, now

inexplicably uses his lips to pantomime the very exaggerated blowing up of a balloon or something, or maybe the oo, oo, oo of a monkey. What Francis would say is that his baby brother Lewis is sitting there resuscitating the monkey in his family.

Francis apes Lewis's monkeyshine. It will take many years from this night for life to finally smother again the monkey that Lewis brought to life in our hero.

FOURTEEN

This chapter break in the middle of Francis's backstory has been provided as a chance for everybody to gird themselves for what they know is coming. I know your narrator won't be squandering this opportunity to put his or her emotional house in order before getting a full horrible dose of what the cosmos spent almost 14 billion years growing capable of when it comes to outdoing itself in forming the worst possible clots of hard luck for laying waste to the better examples of its own handiwork.

CUT TO: DRIVEWAY – MORNING

In a big hurry, Francis and Lewis's dad, an extra successful businessman, backs out of the family driveway, roars off into another day spent setting the world on red fire.

CUT TO: DRIVEWAY – MORNING

Again, the family dad screams out of the driveway and off to work. (The foley artist goes with a slightly disguised lion's roar.) Places to go, as they say. People to see. Things to do.

CUT TO: BEDROOM – WEE HOURS

Three-year-old Lewis, with well-loved stuffed monkey in hand, climbs out of his bed with the *Jungle Book* coverlet on it. He is way too chubby for the well-worn second-birthday pajamas he's wearing with a certain skinny little man-cub on them for calling extra attention by comparison to his improbable compliment of fat and happiness even when sleepy-headed. The year since we saw him last has done nothing but solidify (in a spongy or squidgy kind of way) Lewis's position as the universe's biggest goofball.

It is your narrator's rueful literary duty to mention that star-crossed dinosaurs galore are strewn through the room's super-plenitude of other playthings.

We follow Lewis as he leaves his room and walks down the hall and into ten-year-old Francis's room. When he arrives at the side of his big brother's bed, he is hauled by the seat of his PJs up under the covers his brother has lifted for him and his monkey.

Francis couldn't be less aware that this is his little bedmate's last night on this earth, thanks largely to the false sense of security he was lured into by the pure joy Lewis has spent three years bringing to the family household.

CUT TO: DRIVEWAY – MORNING

Day breaks.

CUT TO: FRANCIS'S BED

Francis is there sleeping like a baby, but no Lewis.

CUT TO: MOM AND DAD'S BED

Mom and Dad are there sleeping like babies, but no Lewis.

CUT TO: BATHROOM

No Lewis, who still isn't quite nighttime potty-trained anyway.

CUT TO: LEWIS'S BED

No Lewis. Like it or not, we stay on the bed's emptiness.

While Francis and his mom and his dad and all of us but me your narrator weren't looking, what can only be described as a crime was taking place. Ok, maybe you could also call it an atrocity, or an act of the utmost dereliction, or an affront to or even an all-out assault on any reasonable sense of how much awfulness can be concentrated in a clot of hard luck.

Whatever you want to call it, here's what it was. After three joyful years spent loafing and dawdling and lollygagging along the developmental trail blazed by the fittest of the apes and then the fittest of the naked apes who came before us, Francis's little baby brother arrived right on time at the well-known milepost where enough of the toddler's natural curiosity and sense of independence have built up for the nipper to pick up the trick of wandering off, or eloping as it's known in the literature.

46

Twistedly our oops baby had come into all the aplomb it takes to catch and act on the travel bug thanks to the utter snugness he himself made his family able to create for him and themselves and utterly unable to recreate when he was gone.

At any rate, the problem with Lewis's being punctually afflicted with an itch in his three-year-old feet is that at this point he was hopelessly behind schedule on the learning curve leading up to the language skills it takes to use your words to tell yourself, even if in only two to five-word little sentences that barely make sense, that you really shouldn't be outside hiding behind your family's car.

CUT TO: WIDE OPEN FRONT DOOR – MID-MORNING

From inside the house we look out at the whole world.

We begin to hear weeping as we

FADE TO: CLOSED BATHROOM DOOR

Behind the door, Francis's mom weeps horribly.

Francis sits stunned at the foot end of his mom and dad's ruffled bed as he listens to his mother's weeping, which for us but not him is blending with the weeping that also nearly killed us back at the Cinderella Inn.

The silver lining is that the motionlessness that Francis learned right there where and when the whole world came to a full and complete stop will go on later in his life to make him a real mover and shaker in the field of artist's modeling.

Francis buries his face in his hands and cries.

CUT TO: CHURCH – INTERIOR

With a heartbreakingly short but not un-chucklesomely wide casket on a stand nearby, a priest delivers his homily for the dear departed. Our hearts go out to him as he does his best to bring solemn scripture to bear on the doing of justice to the memory of the universe's biggest goofball ever.

Francis sits in his Sunday best between his mom and dad in

the first pew. That hardly watchable look on his face has a lot to do with the terrible sensation of the life-drive draining toward empty out of his father.

Angle on Francis's dad. No more places to go. No more people to see. No more things to do.

The baby in the pew behind Francis is being lightly bounced in the arms of her mother as she makes faces and left-handedly flourishes the plaything she has made of her mother's hairbrush. She suddenly smiles widely.

Francis, who is smiling widely at the baby, knows in his heart and his bones and in everything else on and in his person that she is relaying a message to him from Lewis.

Francis's mom elbows him gently so he will turn around in his seat. He does so like the good son he's always been, even though right now his mom has to browbeat him a little because of the smile on his face at a time like this. His mom also takes this opportunity to straighten up his hair and his clip-on tie.

Having wiped the smile off his face, Francis sits like the picture of holy soberness for a minute until the baby conks him on the back of the head with the hairbrush she's just precociously summoned the gross and also fine motor skills to throw at him to get his attention.

Still looking straight ahead, Francis smiles, nods his appreciation for this overture from this infant middleman with so much more hand-to-eye coordination than the three-year-old she's in the service of. The mom Lewis is survived by levels what can only be called a glower at her onetime youngest son's older brother. Unable to help himself, her only remaining boy classically waves across his face a flat hand that erases the offending lightness of heart, so much and so abruptly so as to have a well-known comical effect.

The mom's not sure what to do about this impishness that would so surely have delighted the deceased honoree of these proceedings.

Angle on the church's big bloody crucifixion. Francis sits there thinking of his little brother up there in heaven making Jesus laugh until he pees in his flowing robes, perhaps by showing his so-called savior the new trick within a trick he'd learned only days before being run over—blowing fart sounds out of his arm to replicate the trumpet of a baby elephant as he marches around and around to the imaginary hup two three fours of Colonel Hathi from a certain movie he will never see again unless there are TVs in heaven and VCRs and places to rent or buy movies, which for your information there aren't.

Or perhaps in Francis's mind's eye Lewis is delighting Jesus with the funny scrunched look that played on his face in his last days as he was forgoing the climb up any number of other learning curves in favor of picking up the trick of wiggling his ears like an elephant can like his big brother had learned he could do one lazy Sunday afternoon toward the end of his time with his baby brother.

Anyway, it is very hard for Francis to keep from laughing out loud much less to keep containing the smile he keeps erasing for his mother for the sake of appearances in the house of none other than god.

It becomes much easier to keep a lid on the inappropriate risibility, though, the more he watches what was allowed to happen to the sweet baby Jesus when he grew up. It also helps that the priest has reached the part of the homily where he's protesting way too much about how much perfect mysterious sense in the grand scriptural scheme of things it makes for the Lord to have taken back a bottomless bundle of the joy that's in such short supply in an existence like the one the Lord in question is said to be watching over.

From some unknown somewhere and somewhen we once again begin to hear weeping.

FIFTEEN

Keep thinking about the just mentioned weeping as you avail yourself of this complimentary chapter break to flirt with a full-blown agoraphobic panic by imagining the King-Louis-sized void left behind by the joy our hero's little brother took with him when he was called back up to heaven for some dumb unknown reason.

Now allow the weeping to creep unsparingly into the foreground of your thought.

CUT TO: CLOSED BATHROOM DOOR

Behind the door, Francis and Lewis's mom weeps horribly.

13-year-old Francis sits stunned at the foot end of his mom's and onetime dad's ruffled bed as he listens to his mother's weeping.

This is the house Lewis's former family moved into when the dad quit working. The poor mom, of course, is crying because the dad has gone on to kill himself three so much more than joyless years after he killed his own little boy.

Before Francis buries his face in his hands, we can't help noticing his growing adroitness at remaining utterly motionless.

CUT TO: CHURCH – INTERIOR

A priest we've seen before holds court, this time with a man-sized casket nearby that has exactly no dimensions that might be described as chucklesome.

Francis sits between his mom and Tony in the front pew. You are not allowed to see Tony's face because the acne has struck him by this point in the overall story and I need you to keep being nothing but fond of our hero's life partner. Trust me, his poor face is a mess. Tony would give his left arm all over again to borrow the veil Francis's mother is wearing this time around in her funeral-going.

Suddenly, a three-and-a-half-year-old in a pretty dress causes a small stir when she steps into the front pew and up to Francis and Tony, who together haul her up and onto the spot they've made for her between them. Francis can feel his and Lewis's mom browbeating all three of them through the crepe of her mourning veil.

If you haven't guessed yet, the little rascal with the shit-eating grin on her face because she gets to sit next to her two favorite playmates in the whole world is that super cute message deliverer who conked Francis on the head at his little brother's funeral.

Angle on a man a few pews back. That's the little grinner's dad and also Francis and Lewis's dad's own little brother.

For some unknown reason (for now) we stay focused on the man a while so the banality of him can soak in while a certain presumptive buff of the celibate life stands up there at a certain hallowed Catholic locale that gave its name to the altar boys kneeling there at the service of the celibacy buff in question as he goes on and on about the mysterious ways the Lord works in.

It wouldn't surprise me if your minds are wandering back right now to that glistening bare-naked Greco wrestling standoff where mention was made of a certain boy buff given the pet name of Plato by Ariston of Argos, his Greco wrestling coach.

Enough said for now.

CUT TO: APARTMENT – EVENING

Lewis's aging stuffed monkey is sitting up on an end table next to a well-worn overstuffed sofa.

From the monkey's POV we watch the grown-up Francis and Tony throw themselves in the middle of the living room into the same jazzercise routine Francis had introduced into their lives back when the two were grade schoolers.

You'll be happy to see that it's hard to even tell that Tony, back comfortably into the eight and a half range on the male beauty scale, was one of those whose natural life course had a certain obstacle-course-worth of ugly bumps thrown into it for no good reason.

Anyway, this apartment, Francis and Tony's, is pretty sparsely appointed but not uncozy. I have brought you to this safe space to perhaps unnecessarily say that all those demons to wrestle with (with more still to come) from Francis's past are why Tony thought Francis's inner Hercules might not have been strong enough or even available for shielding Robin from her demons.

Francis and Tony wrap up their jazzercising. With his right hand Francis feels the pulse in Tony's right wrist and Tony feels the pulse in Francis's left one. Both count heartbeats in their sweaty head.

FRANCIS: One-ten.

TONY: One-twenty-five.

Francis gloats.

SIXTEEN

Francis and Tony take a much-deserved load off on their favorite park bench in their favorite spot in the park.

How about we push the pause button on all the sadness. Want to see the best moment of Francis's life, the one he is sitting there reliving for only about the millionth time already?

Close-up of Francis's dreamy face.

>TONY: Thinking about Robin?

>FRANCIS: How could you tell?

>TONY: The noisy little love birdies flying around your head told me.

Francis smiles. Tony smiles.

CUT TO: ART STUDIO

Bare-naked, Francis is laid out on a platform, his head propped up in his left hand. He'd be perfectly reprising Burt Reynolds's iconic nude shoot if he had a lot more facial and body hair and if he was lying on a dead bear and if he was smoking a tiparillo with an ashtray nearby and if he was turned around the other way so it was his right arm propping up his head and if everybody couldn't see his penis because a hairy arm was strategically if not modestly covering it up.

What our hero is doing an even better job of impersonating is the sitting duck he is for all intents and purposes while off-camera little baby Cupid himself is busy drawing a bead on his heart.

Ready. Aim…

Quite unprofessionally, Francis's eyes widen, his jaw drops. He of course has just laid eyes on Robin for the first time— the best moment of his life.

Fire.

Close-up of Francis's bare, unhairy chest in its greatest role as the bullseye into which our boy Cupid is burying every arrow in his quiver.

Close-up of the hopeless lovesickness that has instantly become an inextinguishable feature of Francis's face.

Out of arrows, Cupid has just nailed Francis in the head with his empty quiver. Now he is throwing his ornate bow at our hero's totally exposed groin. Here comes the little crack shot's dirty diaper as one of the slings and arrows of outrageously good fortune. That splash you hear is that unexpectedly well-hung cherub firehosing Francis in the chest with his pee because he's run out of other stuff to strike him with love for Robin with.

His considerable bladder empty, the wiry little naked bastard is now delivering the people's elbow repeatedly to the side of Francis's head. That done, he is kicking Francis in the nuts. Now he is challenging Francis to try whistling while he's undergoing not one but two vicious titty twisters.

Close-up of Francis's poor nipples. We hear Francis whistle under his breath. We are proud of him.

The focus returns to Francis's face. You're getting anxious I bet to see the woman of Francis's dreams. Try waiting 14 post-latency-phase years like Francis did. Anyway, brace yourself. If you're standing up on a treadmill or something, hop off of it and find somewhere to sit down. If you're riding a stationary bike, hop off of it and sit down. If you've got anything in your mouth like a lozenge or a bite from an energy bar or something, swallow it now so you don't choke. Ladies, do not hold it against your man if you know in your heart that he'd go weak-kneed at the sight of the eyeful you're about to see. Single men and lesbian women, do not fight back if Cupid strikes you. I know he's short and sort of doughy, but trust me, resistance against that unbelievably dirty fighter is futile.

Angle on ROBIN. She is truly beautiful in the eyes of any beholder as she stands next to a very old man in a wheelchair parked in front of an easel. Robin watches the palsied wielding of the big fat pencil the old man uses to sketch Francis's now floridly glowing likeness.

So there she is. There's Robin somehow holding up under a beauty so huge that it includes everything that is beautiful in the world.

I know what a lot of you are thinking right now. You're thinking I and everybody else shouldn't be male gazing at this young woman who doesn't deserve to be objectified and one-dimensionalized when all she wants to do is be left alone while Francis is being two-dimensionalized around the room. Trust me, all eight and a half billion of her fellow human beings gazing away at Robin at the same time wouldn't show up on a top ten million list of bad things that have happened to her.

We unapologetically watch Robin look Francis's way. That rhythmic squeaking you hear is Cupid now humping Francis in the ass. I mean, he is really going at it. And you know what? Francis is so transported by that very first locking of eyes with Robin that the humping back there isn't plunging up any of the recently hinted-at bad stuff in his past that we'll be getting into later.

Robin's eyes super demurely go back to the old man's rendering of the man proper.

Angle on Francis. To his infinite discredit, while Robin is watching him come to life on the old man's oversized sketch pad, he is indulging in his pet sex fantasy to help his already-mentioned grower make a better second impression than, say, Michaelangelo's David's grower would have made if it were him lying there sideways on the model's platform.

We cut away all but subliminally to a very elaborate sexual tableau featuring a laurel-wreathed and well-greased Francis ringed Kubrickianly by a dirty dozen kneeling and stark naked vestal virgins trying daintily but failing to eat glazed donuts in one hand and powdered sugar-dusted lemon jellyfilleds in another without making a highly suggestive mess of themselves.

When we return to the art studio, a healthy amount of panic is playing across Francis's face. This is because the fantasy we just left is so smoking hot after so many virgin years spent editing it that suddenly Francis has got a runaway arousal on his hands.

To his credit, he does not break character and pull an emergency Burt Reynolds with the arm that's not busy propping up his head.

To his infinite discredit plus one, though, he resorts to thinking about Lewis's casket so both the mood killing torture of its shortness and the ticklesomeness of its width can put a damper on his flubbed-up posing.

That rubbing sound you now hear is a handful of miffed artist types trying to erase the extra stretch of penis they just sketched only to have it vanish. For Francis's part, he is now praying to god that Robin will not look his way again before he's had a chance to let a dose of softer porn work its less potent magic.

Angle on Robin, who of course looks his way before god has gotten around to answering Francis's simple prayer.

Jesus. Look how much more beautiful she gets every time you see her again.

Believe it or not, she was an ugly duckling. If her own single mother had kept and not thrown out her school photos you could line them up in chronological order and capture the ungainly spectacle of an unassuming waif doing her gawky level best to squirm her way out of the beautiful uncocooning that will only leave her more homeless. You'll see soon enough what I mean by this weird image.

Angle on Tony in the doorway of the studio. He's got hearts galore in his eyes also as he watches Robin. That slapping sound you hear is Cupid flogging him mercilessly about the shins and ankles with his spent cherub's schlong. Tony is being filled with a more platonic (not that kind of platonic) love for Robin, though he is falling in love with her no less than Francis is busy doing on the other side of the room. Just so you know, there's no reason whatsoever to believe that both of our love-struck beholders would not have fallen bottomlessly in love with Robin even if she'd never grown out of her so-called ugly duckling phase.

Robin flips the page on the sketch pad so the old man can start a new rendering of Francis (as opposed to dealing with the capricious penis issue).

I don't want to rain on Francis's best moment, but I have to ask you something. Isn't it really hard to believe that so incredibly beautiful a soul as Robin right there could be the product of the terribly violent gang rape of a poor woman who in all the world was maybe least prepared to raise the product of a violent gang rape?

SEVENTEEN

Still here in the art studio. It's break time. The art students mill around. Robin watches the old man put some finishing touches on one of his drawings. With some intermediate shading techniques, he is doing a decent job of capturing Francis's already mentioned out-of-control glowing.

In a robe, Francis walks quite suavely up to Robin. Throughout the scene that follows, Robin's fragileness is palpable. It would feel so good to give her a hug.

FRANCIS: Hi. I'm Francis, like the Talking Mule.

Robin blushes.

Francis blushes, having perhaps over self-consciously jumped to the conclusion that Robin's blushing because she thinks he's just boasted by association about a well-hungedness.

With nothing better to think of to do with his hands, he holds the right one out to Robin. She shakes it.

ROBIN: I'm Robin.

The old man in a wheelchair extends a hand. Francis grudgingly releases Robin's hand, shakes the old man's.

TOM: Tom.

FRANCIS: A pleasure to meet you, Tom.

He looks over at Robin, smiles, looks back at Tom.

FRANCIS: Sir, could you skooch over a little? Your wife's beauty is making my knees weak, too.

Tom laughs.

TOM: Robin's not my wife.

Francis raises an eyebrow.

FRANCIS: Does Robin's husband know about you two?

Tom laughs again.

ROBIN: I'm not married.

TOM: Robin's my attendant.

Winded, Tony arrives at Francis's side. Behind his back he holds the bouquet Francis sent him out for. Secretly, Tony hands the flowers off to Francis.

FRANCIS: Robin. Tom. This is my attendant, Tony.

Tony smiles, shakes hands with Robin, then Tom.

TONY: Sir, may I just say that if I had a wife as stunning as yours, I would need a wheelchair too.

Francis smiles. Tom and Robin are dumbstruck a little by this echo of Francis's pleasantry.

FRANCIS: Robin is not Tom's wife.

Tony raises an eyebrow.

TONY: Does Robin's husband know about these two?

Francis smiles. Robin and Tom look curiously at one another.

FRANCIS: Robin's not married.

TONY: Does she have a boyfriend?

Francis looks at Robin. Bashfully she shakes her head no.

FRANCIS: These are for you.

Francis hands Robin the flowers. Modestly, she admires his token of hopeless love with downcast eyes. Finally, she looks up at Francis. Her simple smile is nearly as beautiful as she is, if that makes any sense.

Unfortunately, we begin to hear an all-too familiar weeping.

EIGHTEEN

The weeping, of course, is Robin's coming from behind the closed bathroom door of the now familiar room at the Cinderella Inn.

Francis sits stunned at the foot end of the ruffled queen-size bed.

In a perfect world where Aristotle had kept all his pronouncements to himself, I could have gone right into showing you the 28 glorious days that followed that beautiful smile Robin just gave Francis. But if this first act goes on for any longer, it will be impossible to make it exist in the proper golden dramatic symmetry with the two acts to follow.

So to wrap it up, we are back to where the act in question quickly skipped after it began, as you may remember, in the earth's Triassic period—in the immediate aftermath of Francis's demolishing Robin's china shop. I'll have to wait till some appropriate point in Act 2 to show you Robin's and Francis's fairytale four-week courtship. Maybe we'll do it while Francis is in jail for the semi-random act of vandalism he committed when Robin disappeared shortly after this crushing blow.

We watch Francis listen to Robin echo his mother's weepings and vice versa. The candles have burned down a little since we saw them last. The needle still rides the inside of the spinning vinyl.

As it turns out, while Francis is sitting utterly abandoned by his inner Hercules, listening to the weeping that will never not haunt him, Tom, the old man, Robin's employer, with whom she was living in the one and only arrangement in which she could feel truly safe in a world in the bad habit of doing harm to her, is dying of so-called natural causes.

CUT TO: PARK BENCH – MORNING

Francis and Tony sit stunned together in their favorite spot.

Tony sits on Francis's right side. If Imaginary Francis were back to doing the Voice Over duties, he'd use the world's most brutally convoluted tone to say "Welcome to Act 2".

Focus on Tony. He is not saying "I told you so" with respect to Robin's not having been ready to have sex with Francis.

Focus on Francis. He is on the first day of the endless 10 years it will be before he sees Robin again. Tony, of course, will never see her again.

Focus on Tony, who stands up, steps in front of Francis, on whose left side he then sits so he can put his right arm around him.

NINETEEN

On the overstuffed sofa in Francis and Tony's apartment, the former sits stonily before the latter, who paints a widely smiling clown face on our hero. As inappropriate as it is at a time like this, we note that Tony has gotten pretty good with his right hand over the years.

> FRANCIS: Your whole life has just been cold-bloodedly ruined by a faulty article of reconstituted muck from the bowels of Mother Earth. What semi-random act of vandalism do you commit in your boundless outrage?

> TONY: Well, I suppose you could paint Snidely Whiplash mustaches on a pack of oil derricks when they bend over.

Francis nods. The smile under the phony wide smile on his face is decidedly equivocal as Tony finishes up the painting.

You probably recognized just then the germ of the poem "Fucked in the Ass by the Star-Crossed Prophylactadon," which Francis will drunkenly deliver on open mic night in ten years' time. I suppose you could see the whole next decade as simply the process of Tony's not un-Triassic scenario stewing deep down in Francis's creative juices.

CUT TO: BACKYARD BIRTHDAY PARTY – DAY

In full clown costume, Francis bankrolls his impending act of vandalism by making squeaky balloon wiener dogs at a four-year-old's birthday party as a goofy pack of under-fives looks dog-lovingly on. The twist is that Francis is bending and twisting a lot of long Hydra heads onto the wiener dog proper.

In a minute he will scare the birthday boy and his playmates quite a bit when he describes the marshes of Lerna from which the Many-Headed Hydra sprang and when he explains that the Hydra is a symbol of the utter futility of trying to slay the nest of snaky demons that assail us all the time for no good reason.

Francis finishes the wiener dog slash Many-Headed Hydra he's been squeakily working on, hands it to the birthday boy as all the other cone-hatted, sugar-crazed party-goers scream for one just like it. Francis stretches out a long, new, uninflated balloon to loosen it so he can start building the next symbol of the utter futility of resisting all that's arrayed against us.

Even your omniverbal narrator can't tell you how hard it was for Francis not to blow up a bunch of dicks and balls to hand out as symbols of the royal screwing life has in store most likely for each and every one of those poor little snot-nosed knee-high extras in this scene.

A beautiful little kid in the crowd catches Francis's eye.

> KID: Could you make me a monkey?

Francis smiles widely underneath his wide clown smile. What you just witnessed, of course, was Lewis reaching Francis somehow through the thick, dark clouds of his big brother's boundless outrage.

CUT TO: TONY

He sits alone on the curb outside the birthday boy's house. The fear was that his missing arm might scare or overly interest the children or otherwise cut into the focus on the birthday boy.

A series of parked cars each have a bright yellow sign that reads "Caution: Child on Board" in the back window where any oncoming would-be complier with the caution warning won't see it. Of course, any caution sign in the front window would have to be so big for oncoming drivers to see it in time to heed the warning that the driver of a car with such a sign in the front window wouldn't be in a position to see and thereby in a position to heed any caution warnings in the front or the back windows of other cars on the road with a child on board.

CUT TO: BIRTHDAY PARTY

The birthday boy's dad hands Francis a handful of cash as the party winds down behind them.

CUT TO: HARDWARE STORE

With Tony standing next to him, Francis, still in clown outfit, lays down his handful of cash on the check-out counter, on which has been laid his purchase—a very long-handled tool with a collar on the end of it for clamping down on steel pipes that need to be cut through.

> CLERK: You seem pretty happy for a guy with a big plumbing job ahead of him.

> FRANCIS: Good one. The clown guild could use a guy like you.

CUT TO: EMPTY STREET – WEE HOURS

Close-up of the pipe cutter's collar clamped down around the steel neck of a parking meter. We watch the device cut a deepening rut into the pipe as Francis, holding onto the handle for dear life, dead drunkenly walks circles around the meter in what the close reader will recognize as a near visual echo of a certain stuck record. All that's left of the clown outfit on Francis is the red rubber nose playing up how drunk he is.

The severed head falls with a clank to the ground. Francis lovingly places it next to the base. He stands upright. We watch him pick up a half empty bottle of beer from the sidewalk and finish it off from an angle that accentuates the many-headedness of a Hydra-like row of parking meters. From this angle we can also see that Francis has already cut off several other heads. He is really having a Hercules moment.

He stumbles over to the next meter, kisses it tenderly on the head.

64

Angle on Tony sitting several headless meters away on the curb. He's drinking beer, too. He really should not be doing that. In his boundless outrage, he is committing a semi-random act of vandalism against his own internal organs.

Francis, at roughly the same number of RPMs as the stuck record (counterclockwise as opposed to the clockwise direction that Cool Hand Luke walks in when severing meter heads) he walks another series of circles around another meter whose head he's severing.

Believe it or not, in classical Greek mythology, the word "Meter", a nickname for Athena, meant "mother". So in the opening scene of *Cool Hand Luke*, which of course has had a hand, a cool hand if you will, in inspiring the present act of semi-random vandalism by Francis, when star-crossed Lucas Jackson kisses the meter's head before lopping it off, it's like he's kissing the big fat maternal meter of his shitty life.

> TONY (very drunkenly): Here's to Athena.

Tony raises his beer bottle in a toast, and then drains it. At this point it's hard to tell if the toast is a matter of the beer talking or just a dangerously abnormal blood glucose level.

Francis plods his way around the Hydra head.

By "Athena", Tony of course means the virgin deity of the ancient Greeks, worshipped as a goddess of fertility. She is associated with the Aegis, a shield that is a not un-prophylactic symbol of divine protection. She is also known as the guardian of cities. She's doing a heckuva job all the way around.

Focus on the meter's head. Suddenly it topples with a clank to the ground. Francis lovingly places it next to the base.

He sits on the curb, twists the top off another bottle of beer, takes a long swig.

A flood of lights suddenly shines on him. From his POV we make out a cop getting out of a squad car.

> COP: What in the hell are you doing?

Angle on Francis.

FRANCIS (slurring): Maliciously destroying municipal property while under the influence.

TONY: To Athena, guardian of cities.

Francis raises his bottle, smiles widely.

TWENTY

It is Francis's day in court. Tony, now sober and with a blood glucose level approaching normal (for the moment), stands before the female judge with Francis sitting next to him.

> TONY: Your honor. I am here before you today to throw my friend Francis—like the Talking Mule—at the mercy of this fine court. Francis, please rise.

Francis rises.

> TONY: About face.

Francis executes an about face.

> TONY: Clinch.

Francis visibly clinches his buttocks.

> TONY (pointing at Francis's ass): Your honor, let's call this Exhibit A, for obvious reasons, in the case to be made that my friend cum client cum senseless destroyer of municipal property while under the influence is somewhat if not well above average on the callipygianate scale relative to the big beefy male gaze. If need be, your honor, counsel is prepared to call the bailiff to the stand to vouch for the undeniability of this bifurcated cornerstone in the airtight argument we're building here today for leniency.

The judge and the bailiff exchange a look. Both are clearly curious about where this throwing of the defendant at the mercy of the court is going.

> JUDGE: Let's leave the big beefy bailiff out of this, counselor. Continue.

> TONY: Thank you so much, your honor. Now, where was I?

Francis leans over and whispers something in Tony's ear.

TONY: Ah yes. On top of the already-mentioned two sedimentary-rock-hard cornerstones in one, please allow me now to add Francis's butterfingers, the ones that well beyond a reasonable doubt would relegate him constantly to the bent-over position as he went around groping for the soap he dropped again in the crowded shower area. And on top of that let's add the starchy prison food that would leave Francis needing to do countless toe-touchers out there in a yard full of lonely iron pumpers to maintain his girlish figure. I could go on, your honor, but let me get to the point.

JUDGE: Thank you so much, counselor.

TONY: You're very welcome. The point is this: sparing Francis here a stretch in the can so to speak would not only be a matter of showing mercy to the poor soul standing backwards before you here today, it would also spare who knows how many hardened shiv and shank-bearing criminals from fighting over whose girlfriend Francis was going to be.

JUDGE: Are you done?

Tony looks at Francis, who nods his head yes.

TONY: Yes, your honor. I rest my case.

Francis leans over and whispers again in Tony's ear.

TONY: Let the record show that what I meant to say, your honor, is that I rest Francis's case.

JUDGE: Is there anything the Talking Mule would like to say for himself?

Francis looks back at the judge over his shoulder.

FRANCIS: Well, your honor, I guess I would just like to say that when Tony mentioned that "stretch in the can" he could also have chosen "stretch in the roundhouse" and gotten the same point across if you know what I mean.

Francis and the decidedly unsmiling judge lock eyes.

> FRANCIS: Of course, "stretch in the pokey" would
> have gotten the job done too.

The four eyes are locked. Her pair is not failing in the least to
communicate what she thinks about his self-abusing Luke
Jackson brand of sass.

TWENTY-ONE

Francis sits on a cot with his back up against the wall of his jail cell.

Our scofflaw personally composed that stirring (with the accent, of course, on "stir") plea for mercy, which Tony I think delivered magnificently. You are probably beginning to ask yourself, though, why is Francis so preoccupied all the time by penises and sodomy? Your narrator wants you to know, as you watch Francis sit there riding out the first day of this 30-day "stretch in the can," that it is not even semi-gratuitous like the nude scenes have kinda been.

CUT TO: FUNERAL SERVICE

A line of people wait for their turn to view Francis's dad in his casket. One of them, taller than the rest and fraught with a lot more closeted ungodliness, is Francis's paternal uncle, on whom we'd ominously focused for a long moment in an earlier version of this scene. In case you've forgotten, he is the father of the little girl who is sitting off-camera between Tony and Francis as we speak.

Now, I'm no Sigmund Freud, but I think Francis's penis and sodomy fixation might have something to do with his having been raped nine times by his dad's own brother back when he was 11 tender years old. Once it was twice in the same day.

Angle on the dearly departed's only surviving son sitting with his friend Tony and his dead father's three-and-a-half-year-old niece and her widowed aunt, Francis's mother. The camera somehow allows us to see none of the bad acne day Tony is having.

Getting back to Tony's friend Francis, it wasn't eight times he was raped. It wasn't 10. It was nine. On the dot. Nine times. The exact same number as the number of snake heads on the monstrous Many-Headed Hydra I've been talking so much about lately.

Angle on Francis's serial rapist, whose turn it is to view the body. He has somehow already grown larger and more crawling with well-camouflaged awfulness since we saw him last. I know you're no Sigmund Freud either, but nonetheless I leave it to you to draw on what life has personally taught you about the evil men do so you can fill in the gaping blanks I leave in our story in refusing to make myself sick by going into all that has to fall into place in an inner world for the raping of a poor little bereaved kid to happen. I won't be going into all that has to fall into place in the outer world either.

And I don't think I will show you Francis's 11-year-old self being fucked in the ass by his own Uncle Francis no matter how dramatically it would drive home how extreme the prejudice has been against our hero.

No, I'm not going to show dear old Uncle Francis vigorously plunging out of his own nephew's backside the last of any chance he might have had left, after his little brother died and his mom and dad fell apart, of ever becoming a highly successful businessman like the father he'd looked so much up to once was.

Uncle Francis, making a big show of wiping his eyes, returns to his pew.

Want to see the happy place Francis went to in his mind during those nine times?

CUT TO: PARK – DAY

Eleven-year-old Francis sits not unpeacefully alone on a bench in what will soon become his and Tony's favorite spot. This, of course, is also the place young Francis escaped to in his mind when the rapes kept trying unbidden to be relived all over again for some unknown reason.

Like it or not, in the background we hear the sounds of the vigorous plunging proper, or maybe they're the sounds of the stubborn echoes of them.

TWENTY-TWO

We are all crowded now into Francis's jail cell. For his part, he is stretched out on the cot. The not unpeaceful look on his face suggests he might be in a happy place again in his mind.

This might be a good time to show you Robin and Francis's four-glorious-week courtship like I promised.

CUT TO: FLOWERS

It is the beautiful bouquet that Tony gave Francis to give Robin the instant it was ingeniously confirmed that Francis's heart and his gut and his brain were spot on when they told him as one that there's no way the admittedly cruel world could be cruel enough to have his bottomless true love at first sight for Robin be foiled by another man.

Now in a pretty vase, the bouquet has been placed in the center of the kitchen table in Tom's apartment. Robin sits at the table, still visibly disquieted by Francis and his flowers. This disquiet has done nothing to slow down the progress of Robin's growing more beautiful since the last time we were lucky enough to see her. If anything, it has sped the process up.

Tom is asleep in an easy chair in the next room. We also see his oversized sketchpad leaned up against a wall. The coversheet does not allow us to see the topmost of the many sketches of Francis inside. What we can see, though, or at least almost see, or at least think we can see or almost see, is the thin little 60-pound (90 grams per square meter) coversheet over there shuddering under the struggle to hold back the flood of one thousand words per picture all devoted to expressing the same message that Francis loves Robin.

Angle on some woman. We don't recognize her at first, but an involuntary doubletake shows us it's Robin after having grown many times more beautiful. She gets up from the table, goes over and places an afghan on Tom, walks to the shuddering sketchpad, and takes it back to the kitchen table on which she lays it.

It thrums, so much so that Tom's in some danger of being woken up from one of the sweet dreams his sleep has done nothing but feature since Robin became his live-in attendant.

Before our very eyes Robin grows somehow more beautiful as she summons the unheard-of courage to open herself up to the coming bull rush of Francis's love past the lifetime's-worth of defenses that have encased the void whose heartbreaking nature we'll get to later.

Robin takes a deep breath. The heave of her beautiful breasts is barely watchable. (This might be a good time to remember how much Francis loves breasts.)

Before we or Robin are quite ready, she uncovers the first sketch of our hero. It is truly something to watch the love that bull rushes her.

Reverse angle on the picture of Francis blurting a thousand words divided into 333.333 *I love you's*.

CUT TO: ATLAS

As sketched by Tom on the big pad in his lap.

Reverse angle on Francis, who is nakedly straining under the weight of the giant beachball he holds on his shoulders in the middle of Tom and Robin's living room.

Robin sits on one end of a sofa sewing an article of Tom's clothing. On the other end sits Tony. He takes and eats a chocolate from the box sitting between him and Robin.

Robin looks up from her work. A second bouquet has joined the first on the kitchen table.

CUT TO: BEDROOM – NIGHT

In their own apartment now, Tony lies face-up in one twin bed in this smallish room and Francis lies face-up in the twin bed nearby. Francis's hands are folded together on his chest.

FRANCIS: Tony. You are saying your bedtime

prayers for the first time in many many years. You get to the part where you want to offer god something very valuable to you in exchange for his not taking Robin away. What do you offer him?

TONY: Well. Many people in these situations like to offer to give their right arm.

FRANCIS: I thought of that.

TONY: It makes it hard, though, to pray to god anymore after he's taken one of your arms and the hand it's attached to.

Angle on Francis's folded hands.

FADE TO: DARKNESS

An alarm sounds. The alarm is turned off. A light goes on. Francis sits up in his bed. Tony sits up in his. From the nightstand between the two beds, Francis takes up the blood testing instruments. He pricks one of Tony's remaining five fingers, goes about testing Tony's blood sugar level.

TONY: You should feel free to offer god my right arm so he won't take Robin away.

FRANCIS: Thanks. I already offered him your right nut, though, so that when Robin is ready you will have an arm left to put around her.

TONY: Thanks, I appreciate it.

FRANCIS: Of course... Tony.

TONY: Yeah.

FRANCIS: I know your right nut's your favorite, but I felt like I needed to offer god something extra precious.

TONY: It's just that the left one itches so much.

FRANCIS: I know. I know. I'm sorry.

TONY: That's ok. Whatever it takes... Francis.

FRANCIS: Yeah.

TONY: I can't wait to put my arm around Robin.

FRANCIS: It's going to be something.

CUT TO: FLOWERS

Several more bouquets have joined the two we've already seen on Tom and Robin's kitchen table.

CUT TO: BEDROOM

Robin thumbtacks a sketch of Francis on one of the walls of her smallish bedroom. In the sketch Francis simply sits on a piano bench facing the viewer. Somehow, though, Tom has captured just how sweet Francis is on Robin as he sits there motionlessly throwing himself at her.

CUT TO: FRANCIS – LAZY SUNDAY AFTERNOON

His Brylcreemed hair perfectly parted like in the old days, Francis sits fully and dapperly clothed to the left of Robin who sits to the left of Tony on the sofa we earlier saw Robin and Tony sitting on along with the box of chocolates where Robin is sitting now.

We see that of all possibilities, *Cool Hand Luke* happens to have begun playing on the classic movie channel on the television. We watch Luke Jackson tenderly kiss the star-crossed head of the earlier-mentioned parking meter by way of adding extra texture before the fact to the soul-crushing scene between Luke and his mother Arletta later in the show.

The Cupid AKA Eros-struck hero of our story is smile-happily sitting there every bit as drunk on love for Robin as the Letum AKA Thanatos-struck hero of *Cool Hand Luke* is smile-happily punch drunk by now in a life that has turned him into nothing but collateral damage in the fight to the bittersweet end between the winged little shit called the god of death and the unheard of amount of the life force that Luke Jackson was born with for better or worse.

Angle on the hero of our story. All he can think about right now is how to channel the man of action he was once well on his way to becoming so he can put into bold action the game-changing deed of putting his arm around Robin for the first time like he's thought about doing so often and in such fine-grained physical and emotional detail that he's maybe hexed the chance of it ever actually happening in real life.

No sooner does Francis luck into the plan to seamlessly convert a debonair running of his hand over the right side of his perfect hair into an executing of the deed in question than unluckily his own superpower of motionlesslness turns utterly and completely against him.

This is when Tony starts making a show of reaching for a spot on the back of his left side that he can't quite scratch.

> TONY: Hey, Francis. Would you mind giving my chronically itchy left upper rhomboid a little scratch. I still can't quite reach it.

Francis smiles.

> FRANCIS: Leave it to me, old pal.

Francis reaches behind Robin and gives the phantom itch on his old pal's left upper rhomboid a good scratch while Tony lays it on thick with a dog-like twitching of his foot and a preverbal vocalizing of great pleasure.

> TONY: That's good, Francis. And would you mind leaving your hand nearby in case the itch comes back?

> FRANCIS: I guess I could do that for you.

Francis and Tony smile. In a minute, Tony joins his old pal on cloud number nine when he puts his phantom left arm around their gal Robin, who will be joining them soon on the cloud in question when it becomes undeniable that the intimate attentions of the men in question, particularly the one to her left, didn't bring the world tumbling down around her.

This is how our cloud-dwellers will sit for the entirety of

Luke Jackson's slide to the already-mentioned bittersweet end. It will not matter the least little bit to Francis and Tony that their real right arm and their phantom left one respectively keep getting deader by the minute.

Those of you who are familiar with the joculo-brutal Cool Hand Luke story are probably wondering how three life-hammered viewers like our trio there on the sofa could sit through all that the world threw at Luke when he wasn't busy throwing shit back at it.

It's pretty simple. Thanks to the wonders of the cinematic narrative present, the characters in our story are/were sitting there at some level feeling like the immeasurable amounts of energy that god isn't/wasn't spending on doing his job of looking out for poor Luke Jackson are/were being spent on them on this Sunday afternoon, sent to them from heaven.

TWENTY-THREE

No, Robin and Francis's fairytale courtship isn't over. Not yet. The chapter break is meant to make it seem like that *mensis mirabilis* went on for longer than it did.

Anyway, here we all are over the moon ourselves about the beauty of the bouquets proper and all the wonderful things they embody that have continued to proliferate on Robin and Tom's kitchen table. All the many kinds and arrangements of flowers have started collectively taking on the look of what you might find in the room of a convalescing princess who's taken a big turn for the better.

Angle on Francis, who now stands in the middle of the living room nakedly facing down Goliath in his greatest role as Michelangelo's David challenging Tom to find room on his oversized sketchpad for all the suave indomitability his model is exuding.

Angle on Robin, who sits on the sofa and pricks Tony's finger. If I were being literal when I say Tony is gobbling up Robin's sweetness to him, he'd be missing a lot of this moment owing to the diabetic coma he was slipping into.

CUT TO: SKETCHES

Likenesses of Francis in various poses have proliferated on Robin's bedroom walls.

Angle on Robin, who sits on her bed looking at the Polaroid snapshot in her hand. Over her shoulder we look at Tony with his unphantom right arm around Robin and Francis with his left arm around her. All three have obviously just said "cheese", as if they needed to manufacture a smile at a time like this.

Robin looks up. We see a sketch of Francis as Rodin's Thinker. Know what he was thinking? He was thinking about that very snapshot that Robin and we have been looking at. Tom had just taken it for them that morning. It was the second time Tony had ever had his arm around Robin and the third time for Francis. It felt so good for all involved.

Angle on Robin, whose beauty we watch grow as she looks at Tony and Francis with their arms around her. Do not forget this little 3.06 x 3.12 inch keepsake. It becomes hugely important later in our story.

CUT TO: TOM'S APARTMENT – EVENING

Tony sits in Tom's recliner. Tom sits next to him in his wheelchair. A little shakily he pricks Tony's finger.

Behind them bouquets now completely blanket the kitchen table.

Where are Francis and Robin, you ask. They are out on a date.

FADE TO: PARK – DAY

Francis and Tony sit peacefully in their favorite spot. Angle on Francis as he sits there thinking about Robin. Angle on Tony as he sits there thinking about Robin. Angle again on Francis as he sits there thinking about Tony thinking about Robin. Now he's sitting there thinking about Robin thinking about him. And Tony. Angle on both Tony and Francis sitting there seeing Robin's beauty in everything.

Reverse angle on the park. After a moment we focus on a toddler making a monkey of himself on a far-off jungle gym. That of course is Lewis once removed. He wants Francis and Tony to see Robin's beauty in him too, which they do. With a smile.

Shot of the sky. That is heaven shining down on Francis and Tony while time simply passes so the whole world can take on more and more of Robin's growing beauty.

We sit watching time simply pass for a while.

> TONY: So. Did you kiss her?
>
> FRANCIS: Oh yes I surely did. And she kissed me back.

TWENTY-FOUR

CHURCH – INTERIOR

Francis and Tony sit next to each other in the now empty church where we last saw them together at Francis's dad's funeral. Francis's hands are folded in prayer. So are Tony's, though one of Tony's hands, of course, is all in his mind.

The two are fervently reiterating that they will gladly cough up Tony's right nut in exchange for god's not taking Robin away from them. Tony doesn't know it, but Francis is tossing in Tony's already-mentioned itch-prone left nut too to be on the safe side.

In case you're wondering, we are all still in fairytale courtship land. And also, your narrator would like to take this opportunity to apologize for subjecting his dear readers to the image of Tony's right nut being coughed up.

CUT TO: STREET – DAY

Francis and Tony help a little old lady cross the street at a busy rush-hour intersection. They are making super dangerously slow progress, well under the average pedestrian's 3.5 to 4 feet per second. We begin fearing a little for their lives when the WALK interval winds down to zero with them in the dead middle of the street, where ill-advisedly they pause to toy with the idea of turning around and heading back to the street corner they came from.

Do not blame the little old lady for this predicament. The pace has been mostly set by Francis and Tony, who have worn themselves ragged doing good works all day all over town. This, for instance, is the 12th little old lady they have helped to cross this street at this intersection alone.

As the green-lighted cars go hair-raisingly whipping by in both directions, under their breath Tony and Francis mercilessly curse a certain 16th century German *sauertopf* (sourpuss) and precursory Nazi called Martin Luther, who famously moved heaven and earth if you will to take good works on behalf of one's fellow man and woman off the salvation table in favor of a blind faith in god's grace.

When the day started, Robin's new boyfriend and their shared soulmate and best friend Tony were shooting for an even 50-50 split between doing good works and banking on a freshly reborn faith in god's grace to coax the Lord over to the side of not taking Robin away from them like he'd taken a lot of their other cherished things, as the reader well knows.

The more common purslane and petty spurge and jimsonweed they pulled on the neglected grounds of the homeless shelter, though, and the more white bread and bologna sandwiches and apples they handed out at the charity kitchen, and the more sickly smiles Francis clownishly put on the faces of the sweet little innocent kids at the children's hospital, and the more lonely broken-down ladies they helped cross the busy street, the more flashbacks they kept having to the church scene at the end of *Cool Hand Luke* where god has been handed a perfectly good opportunity to make up for botching his job of looking after Luke his whole life and chooses to go a different direction entirely.

So anyway, by close of the business day in question, Francis and Tony's combined faith in their faith in god's grace wouldn't save the least, most sweet and innocent and meek and giving of god's creatures. So they're pouring everything they've got into doing good works and hoping for the best, as opposed, say, to having a good deed like helping a lonely broken-down old lady cross the street be punished by a brush with death in not one but two directions.

Since obviously Tony and Francis survived their punishment for trying to be nice to a perfect little hunched over stranger, allow me to close out this scene by mentioning that Francis got not one laugh and barely even one smile out of that whole big brood's worth of life-hammered old road-crossers to whom very loudly and with perfect enunciation so he'd be heard and understood he posed the question "Why did the good-looking older but wiser chick cross the road?" so he could lighten their and his and Tony's long day by delivering the objectively not un-funny punchline "To catch one gorgeous boytoy for each arm."

CUT TO: BATHROOM

Francis and Tony together lift Tom from his wheelchair and place him on the toilet. No, this simple act of human kindness does not fall into the category of good works.

CUT TO: FLOWERS

Beautiful bouquets are now piled on beautiful bouquets.

Angle on Francis, Tony, and Robin as they jazzercise in the living room.

CUT TO: PARK – DAY

Robin sits between Francis and Tony in their favorite spot. Tom sits next to them in his wheelchair.

We watch the foursome watch the world go by for a while.

> ROBIN: Tony. Do you ever feel pain in your missing arm?

> TONY: All the time. Only I don't feel it because of the ambulatory numbness my diabetes causes in my limbs.

Francis smiles. So does Robin. And Tom. They all go back to watching the world go by.

Do you see why Francis thought Robin was ready to consummate what he had every reason to hope beyond hope would be a pure and simple love story for the ages?

TWENTY-FIVE

At the check-out counter of an antique store, Francis and Tony buy the faulty record player we are all too familiar with.

A sweet song begins playing in the background. It continues through the short medley of scenes to follow. Let's give Imaginary Francis another Voice Over. Warning: Its somberness is going to stand in pretty rough contrast to the tone of the courtship story that's just about over.

FADE TO: CANDLE SHOP

Francis and Tony pick out the romantic candles whose flickering light will soon be casting the saddest shadows of Francis on the walls of the motel room where so much of him is entombed.

> IMAGINARY FRANCIS (V.O.): Your omniscient [sic] narrator and I haven't shown you all the little retreats Robin made as Tony and I were drawing her by inches out of her lifelong hiding place.

GROCERY STORE

Francis and Tony stand in line waiting to pay for sparkling cider.

> IMAGINARY FRANCIS (V.O.): You haven't seen really how much distress her attractiveness caused her in this world from which all but a very few fibers of her being wanted desperately to retire.

FLOWER SHOP

Francis and Tony pay for a dozen red roses.

> IMAGINARY FRANCIS (V.O.): It wasn't until ten years later that I learned just how brave poor Robin was being in allowing herself to blossom a little.

ROOM AT THE CINDERELLA INN – AFTERNOON

We are bringing Imaginary Francis down from his bird's eye view of our story. It's just too hard on the heart to imagine even an Imaginary Francis re-covering the ground we're about to cover.

It's hard enough for your narrator to go over how Francis and Tony showed up on the dot of their early check-in time of two o'clock so they could make sure everything they could control was in perfect order.

We watch Tony position the candles so they're just right. We watch Francis re-position the candles so they're just right plus a little extra. We watch Tony re-re-position the candles so they're just right plus a little extra plus a little extra.

TONY: You have to be really gentle, Francis.

FRANCIS: I know, Tony.

APARTMENT – EVENING

Well-dressed and groomed, Francis with roses in hand stands stiffly submitting to Tony's close inspection.

Almost but not quite satisfied, Tony licks a couple fingers, steps up and spruces Francis a touch with a handsome finger wave. He steps back, gives the flourish a once over, nods his satisfaction.

Imagine that while you were watching the above, I myself was talking to you all in the following Voice Over.

NARRATOR (V.O.): What Francis didn't know on the eve of his and Robin's consummating their love for each other, and what Tony mercifully will never know, is that Robin's whole life up to the point of meeting Francis and Tony had really been nothing at all but a putting in place of the conditions that would make a faulty condom the worst possible thing that could happen to her.

CUT TO: CINDERELLA INN

Focus on the closed bathroom door.

84

Reverse angle on the queen-size bed. In the romantic light of the extra extra perfectly positioned candles, with the world's most beautiful song playing on the record player, a happy, bare-chested Francis sits with his lower half under the covers as he waits for Robin.

> NARRATOR (V.O.): What Francis found out only recently in real time is that in the long aftermath of Robin's brutal conception, her poor mom, who had been horribly disfigured in the gang rape that produced the love of Francis's life, devoted herself single-mindedly night and day to impressing upon her ugly duckling daughter that the filthy genes she was carrying everywhere inside her needed never to contaminate anybody else with their filthiness.

Robin emerges from the bathroom. She is too beautiful to be believed in the nightie she is wearing.

She walks in the candlelight up to the bed. Gracefully she gives away none of the great pains her mother has spent twenty-some years taking to keep a moment like this from ever unfolding.

Robin removes the nightdress. Imagine how beautiful her bared breasts must be if they're many times more beautiful than Francis could ever have imagined.

The music stops. From the future relative to this moment in our story we hear crying as Robin bravely drapes her gown over the bedside table before getting into bed with poor Francis.

TWENTY-SIX

Welcome to the halfway point of our story.

More specifically, here we are in Francis's jail cell where he lies on his cot doing the crying that cast such a pall on the end of Chapter Twenty-Five. More specifically still, it is the first Sunday of Francis's incarceration.

Angle on his cellmate, a tattooed brute whose huge beefiness barely fits on his cot. To his credit, he is clearly saddened by Francis's crying. In fact, thus far, he has not quite had the heart to rape Francis, or even to make him suck his cock, which is quite large by the way. If you asked Francis, he'd a little confusingly say that in some not un-platonic way he was still the bitch of this big habitual harm-doer to his own fellow human beings.

Angle on Francis, who's still crying. Let me show you why.

CUT TO: VISITING AREA

Tony, sitting across a table from Francis, is a wreck. A horrible low-grade disorientation is written all over him. Or maybe stamped all over him is a better way to say it. Francis is doing his best to suppress a sob. God only knows, as they say, where Tony's blood sugar level is.

Paul, their psychiatrist friend, was going to stay with Tony for the whole month. But then, as Tony just told Francis in so many words, thanks to a little clot of hard luck, out of nowhere Paul had a stroke.

Francis reaches out a hand to console and be consoled. Tony takes it. A guard glares, shakes her head no. They pull their hands back.

> FRANCIS: Can you spend visiting hours with Paul?

> TONY: I'll try that.

Francis has to collect himself before speaking again.

> FRANCIS: Make sure you keep exercising.

TONY: Ok, I will.

Francis of course is flashing back to the shell of poor worn-out Luke Jackson when the bosses break him in those scenes where they keep making him dig and undig a hole and keep hitting him and hitting him till he whimpers out a pitiful begging for them to stop.

In the medley of scenes to follow, we faintly hear the "Plastic Jesus" song that Luke Jackson sat on his prison bunk and sadly sang along with his unutterably unrushed banjo pluck-strumming after getting word that Arletta had died. Here are the lyrics in case you don't remember them or never heard them in the first place. Read them real slow, with a couple of long pauses. And with a tear in your right eye if you can manage it.

I don't care if it rains or freezes

As long as I got my plastic Jesus

Sitting on the dashboard of my car.

Comes in colors pink and pleasant

Glows in the dark 'cause it's iridescent.

Take it with you when you travel far.

Get yourself a sweet Madonna

Dressed in rhinestone on a

Pedestal of abalone shell.

Goin' 90 I ain't scary

'Cause I got the Virgin Mary

Assuring me

That I won't go to hell.

Get yourself a sweet Madonna

Dressed in rhinestone on a

Pedestal of abalone shell.

Goin' 90 I ain't scary

'Cause I got the Virgin Mary

Assuring me

That I won't go to hell.

Speaking of the Virgin Mary, I forgot to mention that for full effect you should also keep bearing Luke 1:37 in mind as we watch Tony go godforsaken in the scenes to come. And by Luke 1:37, of course, I mean the Bible verse alluded to by the 37 seen repeatedly like a bitterly ironic kick-me sign there on the back of Luke Jackson's prison uniform. The verse goes, "For nothing will be impossible with god", and its original intention was to keep the Virgin Mary keeping the faith after Gabriel let her know about the immaculate knocking of her up.

FADE TO: HOSPITAL ROOM

Tony, looking worse yet for the wear of the little time that's passed since his visit to the county jail, sits in a chair next to Paul's bed. If there were anyone or anything he could beg to stop hitting him he would surely do it.

Angle on Paul. His right side out of commission, he fumblingly lends the efforts of his left hand to those of Tony's right in the preparation of a syringe for delivering Tony's insulin.

CUT TO: STREET – DAY

A homeless person does her inexpert and shaky best to tie Tony's tie for him.

CUT TO: AUDITORIUM

Tony sits in a folding chair nearly prostrate with emotion.

This is Tom's memorial service. That is not only grief, though, that is working Tony over. Now might be a good time to mention that starting in his early twenties, Tony was attacked on and off by this terrible anxiety monster. It was like a screaming wild dog that invaded his system and turned all his particles into a mob of bleating sheep needing crazily to bolt in every direction.

And no, Robin did not attend Tom's memorial.

CUT TO: APARTMENT – NIGHT

In the middle of the living room, Tony abjectly weeps his way through his and Francis's and for a short time Robin's jazzercise routine.

Come to think of it, the anxiety attacks were more like periodic hysteria bombs that went off at his core and he had to somehow keep all his atoms from being scattered by it.

Angle on Lewis's monkey, which sits on the sofa. We watch Tony raise the heart rate that Francis won't be there to check when the workout is over.

CUT TO: BEDROOM – NIGHT

Tony lies face-up on his bed.

The magic that held him all together has started unraveling.

Focus on Tony's silently moving lips. For the illiterate with respect to lip-reading, this is Tony one-handedly praying to god that the thread of whatever it is that explained his being wouldn't slip the rest of the way through his fingers.

CUT TO: SOFA – DAY

Tony sits looking like a general rampant scattering waiting to happen.

In other words, this is Tony one-handedly holding on for dear life to the thread of whatever it was that explained his being. It is Sunday, visiting day at the jail. He wants so badly to go visit Francis, but as you can see he has his hand full.

Angle on Lewis's monkey sitting next to Tony.

Paul said Tony's anxiety attacks were caused by the trauma of losing his arm. And by his dad's giving him diabetes. And by his dad's subsequent alcoholism. And by his mom's having gone half crazy. Maybe more. No. Definitely more. I'm sure his three-year pitched battle with acne at a particularly fragile time of his life didn't help matters either. If you ask me, knowing Tony like I do, he personally took on enough of his life partner Francis's traumas that they also help explain how bad he felt. And let's not forget the extra-added anxiety-causing traumas of the anxiety attacks themselves.

Getting back to the larger cosmic context of our story, and dipping into the much much smaller context, let's frame the periodic falling of Tony apart like this: A certain grossly misnamed factor in the equation called Tony's own Sympathetic Nervous System relentlessly kept putting him on such high alert that loudly and clearly he was picking up the nerve-jangling static noise of the Cosmic Background Radiation that since the all-scattering Big Bang had been waiting to crazily jangle his nerves to simulate the further nerve-jangling sound of a bundle of quantum jitters threatening to jitter itself into a million pieces times near infinity.

Angle on the bundle of jitters.

At any rate, what Tony needs right there and right then is for someone to hold him for a long time. So his body and his mind will remember how to hold everything together.

CUT TO: STREET – EARLY HOURS

A homeless person pricks Tony's shaky finger for him.

CUT TO: HOSPITAL ROOM

Tony, barely holding on, sits next to Paul, who is sound asleep. Quietly and of course with one hand, Tony blows his own nose. He has caught a bad cold, probably because of spending so much time in the hospital with Paul.

TWENTY-SEVEN

Tony sits on a curb again. This time it's outside the grounds of the county jail. It is the day Francis is due to be released, having paid his debt to society. Tony is wracked by a bad coughing jag.

It is hard to calculate how many years Paul's stroke took off Tony's life.

I trust it's occurred to you by now that Francis and Tony were almost as fragile as Robin was. Don't feel bad if it hasn't. I may have left the wrong impression that Tony and Francis had just been breezing through the adult years leading up to the great but fateful day they met Robin.

Tony's now sitting there shivering, calling no end of quantum jitters to mind.

It is true that Tony's settlement from Ganesh Fix-It (thanks to the much earlier-mentioned stamping of the company name on a certain big-ass flying monkey wrench) kept the wolf from Tony and Francis's door, the apartment attached to which it also paid the rent on. And, of course, it must be said that Francis wasn't half bad at generating mad money.

Still, as much as anything else, what the next ten years would go on to show Tony and Francis from the Cinderella Inn scene forward is just how flimsy all along were their defenses against the stone-cold truth that "nothing will be impossible with god" when he's on a mission to ground your flights of enthusiasm for some unknown reason.

CUT TO: PARK – DAY

Francis and Tony sit in their favorite spot, Francis with his arm around Tony, who luckily for us and him and Francis now seems to be in no danger of flying apart.

Reverse angle on the world. All in all, it looks about the same as usual.

TONY: I hope Robin's all right out there.

FRANCIS: Me too. I can still hear her crying.

TONY: I can hear you hearing it.

Three punks come into view, walk up to Francis and Tony.

PUNK: Get a room, you fucking queers.

We kinda hope but also kinda don't hope that Francis and or Tony smarts off to these mean-looking henchboys of whatever the universal forces are that have been put in charge of delivering the kicks we are visited with when we are down.

FADE TO: PARK – DAY

Francis and Tony still sit in their spot. One of Francis's lips is busted. Tony's nose is bleeding.

FRANCIS: Awfully nice of those fellas to go easy on us when they saw you only have one arm.

TONY: Awfully nice. Hope they didn't catch my cold.

FRANCIS: I probably shouldn't have smarted off to them.

TONY: It was probably the hardened jailbird in you talking.

Francis nods, takes a test strip, dips it in the blood from Tony's nose, inserts it in the tester.

FRANCIS: So, how do you suppose the prophylactic factory goes about conducting product testing?

TONY: Well, it probably involves some especially durable girl and boy or boy and boy crash dummies that can withstand the crushing blow of a broken rubber.

Francis nods, prepares the syringe.

CUT TO: BEDROOM – NIGHT

Tony lies face-up in bed. Francis does the same in his.

FRANCIS: Thinking of Robin?

TONY: Yeah. You?

FRANCIS: Yeah.

We watch the two thinking of Robin for a while. We assume that at some point Francis is thinking of Tony thinking of Robin and Tony is thinking of Francis thinking of her.

TONY: I guess god didn't want my right nut.

FRANCIS: Tony. I offered god your left nut too.

TONY: So did I. And my penis.

FRANCIS: You offered god your penis?

TONY: Yeah. Toward the end there.

Francis thinks this over for a moment.

FRANCIS: Why didn't I think of that?

Shame on you if you're thinking that Francis didn't think of Tony's penis because he was too busy thinking about his own penis in the lead-up to stupidly inserting it into a certain booby trap. Of course, this is what Francis is there thinking right now, but still, shame on you for thinking it too.

CUT TO: ART STUDIO

Francis sits naked up on a well-lighted, slightly raised platform. He is reprising his unforgettable role as Rodin's Thinker for a roomful of art students who for their part are thinking that Rodin's Thinker is probably thinking about the guy who gave him the fat lip.

Here's what Francis is really thinking: "I wish I at least had that snapshot of Robin with me and Tony putting our arms around her. If I could only hold onto her beauty captured like that in one moment in time, she would stop getting so debilitatingly more beautiful in my mind while she's out there getting even more beautiful than that in real life."

Angle on a student's rendering of the thinker in question. That little chugga chugga you hear in the background is the train of thought that will lead Francis soon to the debilitating conclusion that even a snapshot of Robin probably gets more beautiful between loving looks at it. It also debilitatingly dawns on him that the snapshot of Robin in question would likely grow more debilitatingly beautiful right before his eyes as he tried but failed to look away from the growing beauty that was so utterly debilitating him.

Angle on our thrice debilitated artist's model.

CUT TO: PARK - DAY

Francis and Tony sit in their spot. Please forgive them their predictability in repairing if you will to the same place all the time to heal their various wounds.

Next to Francis, who sits in the middle, sits Paul. Though we can't quite hear what he's saying, we see that he is throwing himself, deadened but repairing right side and all, into telling Francis and Tony something while the squeezing of a tennis ball with his off hand spontaneously synchronizes with the spitting of big words out of his half compromised mouth.

Francis and Tony graciously nod now and then even though they're not listening to Paul mining the Diagnostic and Statistical Manual of Mental Disorders from memory to formulate a theory about Robin's leaving and not coming back.

Tony and Francis are not really listening not only because what Paul is saying is too complicated for them to follow while being so distracted by thoughts of Robin but also because for them Robin is too perfect in every way for the DSM to apply to her.

It occurs to Tony and Francis at almost exactly the same time that what Paul should be doing is scouring the DSM for the fancy name to give whatever outrageous psychological problem it is that explains a god and or a cosmos givething two relatively decent human beings a thing as perfect as

94

Robin and then takething her away.

CUT TO: LIVING ROOM

That is where Tony and Francis really should be jazzercising.

Angle on Francis and Tony and Lewis's monkey sitting on the sofa.

TONY: Doesn't look like Robin's coming back, does it?

FRANCIS: No.

TONY: Maybe we should go look for her.

FRANCIS: That's a great idea, Tony. And after that we can look for your arm. And then we can look for my little brother and my dad and your healthy pancreas and your mom's sanity and my mom's reason for living and your dad's sobriety and my anal virginity and Robin's regular virginity and my career as a very successful businessman. I'm sure a lot of that stuff has just slipped behind the refrigerator.

Focus on Francis, who's beating himself up for beating up on Tony. He looks over at Tony, who looks very sad.

FRANCIS: I'm sorry. I forgot to mention your career as an air guitarist.

TONY: That's ok, Francis. You've got a lot on your mind.

TWENTY-EIGHT

There's our hero naked and on all fours under a bright spotlight.

No, this is not him looking everywhere for his anal virginity. This is your not un-artistic narrator's rendering of what Francis always looks like to the universal forces of forcible intercourse.

All joking about rape aside, believe it or not, this is the position Francis has been asked to assume at the art studio on the first anniversary of the last time he and Tony saw Robin.

As a little footnote, the money Francis is earning here will all go into paying for the replacement of those heads on that metaphorical Hydra Francis tried to slay in his outrage over losing Robin.

CUT TO: LIVING ROOM

After a moment's worth of thinking we can almost hear Tony and Francis's favorite jazzercise song, the camera moves over to Francis and Tony and Lewis's monkey sitting together on the sofa.

They are looking at least a year older than the last time we saw them.

And speaking of time, it has made no progress at all in healing the wounds of our grieving threesome. That is, unless you count negative progress.

And briefly going back to that thing about the "grieving threesome", I really probably should have found room in the earlier flow of the story to show you how well Robin and Lewis's monkey hit it off.

CUT TO: ART STUDIO

As the Virgin Mary, Francis, in flowing robes and headdress, sits lachrymosely holding a naked and very dead-looking Tony in his lap.

Don't worry. I'm not showing you this pieta to suggest that Francis is a Marian figure. We all know that he wasn't a virgin ten times over. And I'm also not suggesting that Tony's any kind of Christ figure.

Focus on Tony's lifeless face. (You can hardly see the acne scars.) For one thing, Tony's only 32 here, not 33. For another thing, Jesus got out of here with a grand total of like 109 wounds, not counting the dumb ones he probably gave himself in his life as a carpenter. Tony there has already racked up tens upon tens of thousands of pricks just on the fingers of one hand. And he's got about seven or eight thousand to go before he dies in Francis's arms on the tenth anniversary of the last time he ever saw Robin.

The camera pulls back to take in Tony's whole lifeless figure.

Anyway, the reason I'm showing you this is that I think it captures the almost totally debilitating lovesickness that Tony and Francis (and Lewis's monkey, not shown) did their best to nurse each other through over those relentless ten years.

CUT TO: SOFA

Francis, Tony, and the monkey sit together looking individually and collectively overworked. They are winding down right after that foreshadowing you just saw of Tony's terrible death.

>FRANCIS: Tony. You have a gray hair growing on your nuts.

>TONY: I know.

More winding down.

>TONY: I really miss Robin.

>FRANCIS: Me too.

More winding down.

>FRANCIS: Tony. Are you thinking what I'm

thinking?

TONY: That if I pluck the gray hair on my nuts, two more will grow back?

FRANCIS: No, you beautiful silver fox you. I'm thinking we should go look for Robin.

Tony beams.

TONY: Great idea, Francis. I wish I had thought of that.

TWENTY-NINE

Like best overstimulated buddies on a field trip to the
planetarium, Tony and Francis and Lewis's monkey sit next
to each other on a Greyhound bus venturing out there into the
wide world where Robin is calling out to our newbie
travelers with a voice that grows sweeter with each mile they
feel like they're shaving off the distance between them and
the reason the three so thoroughly confirmed homebodies are
braving the wide world in question.

More specifically the bus is heading toward San Francisco,
where Robin grew up according to her herself. This is the one
and only lead scared up by our Greyhoundian sniffers out of
the whereabouts of the beautiful source of the spoors
growing more and more fragrant the closer our practically
baying love hounds get to the Golden Gate City.

Check that. The action plan for reclaiming the heavenly
benison that was takethinged away from them is also
informed by Paul's airtight expert opinion that Robin would
surely return to the most familiar ground possible when her
current locality in the wide world was turned upside down.

Angle on the crazy faces Francis is making.

Reverse angle on the baby aping Francis's faces as her mom
lightly bounces her in the aisle seat just ahead of our trio. Of
course, who you are looking at is none other than Lewis
going along for the ride.

Long shot of the bus on the road to The Golden City.

CUT TO: DOORSTEP – DAY

Back at Francis and Tony's apartment, in the sixth year of
their terrible separation from Robin, she stood right there
sobbing and knocking on the door. Of course, Francis and
Tony weren't inside. They were looking for her in San
Francisco.

CUT TO: PARK – DAY

Francis and Tony's and for a short while Robin's bench is empty.

This is where Robin, with her and Francis's son Henry, like the Navigator, sat for a long time when they did not find Francis and Tony at their old apartment. If they had just been there, Tony would not have died. (Unless, of course, he'd gotten hit by a bus for no good reason or struck by lightning or crushed by a falling piano or fallen to his death in a sinkhole or something.)

Many other bad things wouldn't have happened either. Some other bad things still would have happened, though.

CUT TO: BUS STATION – DAY

A Greyhound bus pulls in. It seems exhausted somehow.

FADE TO: EXHAUSTED-SEEMING GREYHOUND BUS

Along with a lot of other bedraggled passengers, Francis and Tony exit, Lewis's monkey dangling from the little hand Tony's holding.

These are our sleuthhounds returning home after two years'-worth of coming up empty in The Golden City. There's no need to show you those two years.

No need to show you the zero number of times in all their pavement-pounding they turned a corner and there she was. No need to show you the same number of times they looked up from their head-hanging after another long hard day of pavement-pounding and there she was.

No need to show you the zero amount of good it did to ask every old and new street person in San Francisco if they'd seen the most beautiful woman in the world go by or the zero amount of good it did to slow their pavement-pounding down in case she happened to be coming up on them from behind or speed their daily pavement-pounding up in case she was just out of eyesight up ahead.

No need to show you the zero number of days Robin's absence from Francis and Tony's lives didn't grow larger and larger and more and more like the only void in the whole universe that nothing comes rushing into. Or show you the zero amount of difference there was between Francis and Tony's looking all over hell for Robin on her native soil and Francis's once conjured up image of poking around behind a refrigerator for the biggest things missing in our lives.

I'm sure you already know, so I won't bother right now, in other words, to show you how darn good god is at turning around and taking away what he gives us.

CUT TO: PARK – DAY

Francis and Tony sit in their favorite spot as we all approach the moment that broke them.

Reverse angle on the windy day. We see a breeze-borne sheet of paper wafting about evocatively.

Angle on Francis and Tony being buoyed a little by the seeming auspiciousness of this instance of litter being spirited here and there so gracefully by these breaths of wind.

Angle again on the paper. As it unhurriedly rides the lightly playful currents toward Francis and Tony, we listen to Imaginary Francis's Voice Over.

> IMAGINARY FRANCIS (V.O.): It wasn't the relentless speculation that one more session of pavement-pounding up and down the streets of San Francisco would have brought Robin back to us that finally proved too much for us to handle. It wasn't the nonstop actual echo of Robin's crying behind that bathroom door combined with Tony's all-but audible imagining of it. It was not the overcast afternoon that Paul explained pro bono to Tony that his dad was only doing to his own poor liver what he'd done to his own son's pancreas by giving him that virus. It was not the very last of those brutal Thanksgivings we spent at my poor mom's house with my Uncle Francis in it. It was not the day Tony's mom lost track all together of who Tony was. It was not the

gratuitous cruelty of my having to sew the rip that appeared in the seam keeping Lewis's monkey's left arm attached to his body. It was not even the most recent hysteria bomb that went off deep in poor Tony's core.

The paper grows playfully closer.

Angle on a smiling Francis and Tony. Suddenly a gust of ill wind plasters the paper to Tony's face. We see the smile vanish from Francis. We assume the same has happened with Tony.

> IMAGINARY FRANCIS (V.O.): That was the last straw right there. That, of all things, is what did it.

THIRTY

In the living room of the dumpy apartment they moved into upon returning from San Francisco, Francis and Tony, beer bottles in hand, belt out a disco song while Lewis's monkey sits on a crummy sofa watching them drunkenly doing their jazzercise.

CUT TO: BUSY SIDEWALK – MORNING

In white face, an already very drunk Francis mimes the draining of an entire bottle of liquor. Then he actually throws up.

CUT TO: FRANCIS – DAY

In full clown outfit, Francis walks with Tony into a bar.

CUT TO: BIRTHDAY PARTY

A handful of kids play with the sets of dicks and balls Francis has made for them out of balloons.

CUT TO: BEDROOM – NIGHT

Tony, drunk, lies face-up on his twin bed. Francis, drunk and wearing a red clown nose, does the same on his.

> FRANCIS (slurring): So, Tony. The room is spinning, making you feel like you're being flushed down a toilet. How do you make it stop?
>
> TONY (slurring): What hemisphere are you in?
>
> FRANCIS (slurring): Pretty sure it's the north one.
>
> TONY (slurring): I guess then you could drink a shitload of Australian beer so the spinning will go in the opposite direction, cancelling out the spinning you're currently experiencing.

Francis smiles.

CUT TO: CONVENIENCE STORE – NIGHT

Francis and Tony stand outside drinking a shitload of

Australian beer.

I'm pretty sure Paul would say this is Tony doing to his poor liver what his dad's done to his own poor liver for what he did to his son's poor pancreas.

FADE TO: DARKNESS

Francis and Tony's alarm goes off. In the darkness we watch them both soddenly sleep right through it.

CUT TO: PARK – DAY

Francis and Tony sit on their bench. Francis has a shiner and a busted lip. Tony's showing similar signs of having been in a nasty fight.

By their posture you can tell they are on the wagon. That shiner and fat lip Francis got from Tony. When his blood sugar level dipped below 40, his belligerent inner Hercules really came out. Lucky for Tony he's missing his best arm. Otherwise, Francis could never have subdued him in time to get some sugar into his system before he slipped into a coma.

Tony gingerly feels the goose egg on his head, looks down at his busted knuckles, looks over at Francis's face.

> TONY: Wow. That must have been some fight.

> FRANCIS: Oh, yeah. You should have been there.

Francis dips a test strip in the fresh blood on one of Tony's busted knuckles.

CUT TO: DRESSING ROOM

Naked, Francis and Tony take turns hitting a bottle of wine pretty hard to numb the pain of their having fallen hard off the wagon.

CUT TO: ART STUDIO

Angle on a sketch of Francis and Tony in a wrestler's clinch again.

> FRANCIS: Bacchus.

TONY: Dionysus.

FRANCIS (louder): Bacchus.

TONY (even louder): Dionysus.

Angle on the face of the art student, who has suspended his drawing to look agape at the two subjects of his sketch as they argue over which god would take the Olympic laurel wreath in the age-old contact sport of hitting the bottle.

Reverse angle on a well-greased Tony and Francis, who have come unclinched.

FRANCIS: Bacchus.

TONY: Dionysus.

FRANCIS: Bacchus.

TONY: Bacchus.

FRANCIS: Dionysus. D'oh.

Playfully angry over playfully having pretended to fall for the oldest trick in the book, Francis launches into a phony but very rough and tumble big time wrestling match with Tony.

CUT TO: PARK – DAY

Francis and Tony sit on their bench. Tony's arm is in a full cast that goes up past his elbow.

On the wagon.

CUT TO: BAR

Off the wagon, Tony sits very drunk at a table. We see Francis heading to the can. Tony's cast won't let him bring the beer bottle to his mouth like Francis has been doing for him for a good long time judging by the draft if you will of dead soldiers on the table. So Tony pours the beer in with limited success from overhead until he's fallen out of his chair with no arm available for breaking his fall.

CUT TO: PARK – DAY

Francis and Tony, looking like death warmed over, sit

watching the world go by on its way toward the fast-approaching moment they fall again off the wagon they're sitting on as if with the wind blowing through their hair and their knuckles whitening as they hold for dear life onto a super wily sobriety.

FRANCIS: Tony.

TONY: Yeah, Francis.

FRANCIS: Please do not ever forget to remember to leave all remaining limbs inside when riding in a fast-moving vehicle like the runaway wagon of sobriety.

TONY: You got it, old pal.

Francis forgets to not be reminded of that first time he stuck a limb of his out there and put it around Robin while riding the train of his love for her on the way to the crash it was running late for.

CUT TO: APARTMENT – DAY

Francis and Tony, both wearing one of those conical party hats with a rubber band chin strap, sit drinking beer on the crummy sofa they landed on when they fell off the wagon. Tony's arm is no longer in a cast and is not grossly over-pale and extra hairy looking, which is narratorial shorthand for "a good number of weeks have passed."

Angle on Lewis's monkey sitting next to them. He also wears a party hat, a little homemade fez that makes it look like the boys invited an organ grinder to the party. Or a greyhound jockey. Given what Tony's been doing to his poor organs and given the rides on the Greyhound our party monsters have recently taken, you can imagine the verbal monkeying around that has gone on before we all crashed the party.

Anyway, this is the day Francis turned the same age his father was when he walked into the family garage and killed himself with his own idling car.

CUT TO: PARK – DAY

Francis and Tony, still wearing party hats, sit on their bench drinking beer from bottles in brown paper bags.

And no, the cones on their heads are not shorthand for "this is still Francis's birthday." This is almost a whole week later. If you'd asked Francis and Tony separately about this stretch of time, they'd eerily both have said it involved a helluva lot of hops but not one hop onto the wagon.

CUT TO: PARK – MOONLESS NIGHT

Francis and Tony, now wearing quite cockeyed party hats, drink beer without bothering with the paper bags.

Even in the dark they can see Robin's enormously grown and still growing absence in everything.

CUT TO: FRANCIS'S BED

Tony is fucking Francis in the ass, one time, for comfort. That's all I'm going to say about it, except that at least Tony didn't die a virgin. And also maybe to mention that the beer bottle practically glued to Tony's one free hand left him no way to give our hero the reach-around he would have gladly given him under other circumstances.

Ok, fine. I'll also mention that all the sponge baths Francis had to give Tony when his arm was in a cast very likely set the stage for this consummation of their platonic love for one another.

THIRTY-ONE

Our two incredibly spent lovemakers sit at a table at a diner, their stacks of pancakes going untouched in front of them. Francis stares half catatonically into space.

A baby at the next table is making crazier and crazier faces the longer Francis keeps looking right through Lewis.

CUT TO: TINY AND UNTIDY KITCHEN – DAY

Angle on Tony holding a bottle of wine by the neck at a four-person table blankly watching Francis sit staring blankly at a blank tablet on the table in front of him.

Where we are time-wise is one week before the tenth anniversary of the last time they ever saw Robin. Looks like Tony's got a little touch of writer's block. He's supposed to be helping Francis write the first draft of the poem Francis will recite on the night Tony dies.

Tony takes a big swig from the bottle.

Angle on Francis. He watches Tony, who, with his eyes closed, is collecting himself to the best of his ability. Francis snaps out of his distraction as he watches Tony do his already mentioned best to snap out of the distraction still left after the really big hysteria bomb was dropped on him two days earlier.

Francis begins writing on the tablet. I'm almost perfectly sure it was his fresh efforts to help Tony reverse the effects of the big explosion in question that inspired him at first to poetically trace the origins of all his and Tony's troubles all the way back to the Big Bang.

CUT TO: DRUGSTORE

Francis and Tony, cockeyed, stand at the checkout counter watching a box of condoms make its way on the conveyor belt toward the clerk. When it arrives, the clerk takes the box and scans it.

FRANCIS (to the clerk): Young man, are those the very smallest condoms you have?

CLERK: I think so.

FRANCIS: I think I'm going to need to buy a little belt then.

Francis stops in his tracks, looks intently at Tony, who looks intently back at him.

FRANCIS AND TONY: Did somebody just say "a little belt"?

Of course Tony and Francis say "You're jinxed" at the same time and keep doing so until an "ahem" in so many words comes from the next person in line.

CUT TO: BAR

Francis and Tony stand at the bar indulging themselves in "a little belt."

CUT TO: TINY AND UNTIDY KITCHEN

Francis and Tony sit again at the table. Francis blows up a condom, ties it off when it gets very large.

He holds the inflated condom out toward Tony and hands him an unsheathed safety pin.

FRANCIS: Would you care to do the pricking for a change?

For Tony and Francis, this question almost but doesn't quite dredge up the recent drunken love scene between them. It does for us, though, who have fewer reasons not to go there.

TONY: Thought you'd never ask.

Francis clears his throat, holds up and consults the sheet of paper on which the Big Bang poem is written.

FRANCIS: Yada yada, blah blah blah—Ok, here we go: "…and the popping of my bubble that was 14 billion years in the making".

Tony pops the condom.

> FRANCIS: "The Big Bang Heard Round My World".

Both seem reasonably satisfied with their efforts.

CUT TO: TINY AND UNTIDY KITCHEN

Francis and Tony sit again at the table, both doing your narrator a big favor by holding a bottle of hard liquor by the neck that lets the reader know the death spiral is escalating.

They're back at the old drawing board. Here, let me show you why they decided to shit-can the Big Bang draft. Trigger alert: an innocent little kid is about to be hard used for no good reason by the universe.

CUT TO: SIDEWALK – DAY

We see a mom and a dad and their innocent little kid on the sidewalk. For no apparent reason the poor little kid trips. There is no unapparent reason for it either. The oversized dinosaur-shaped backpack the boy's wearing seems to be having its way with him as he cries miserably on all fours. The mom and dad, who have had another long day in a long line of them leading to more long days to come, just stand there waiting for the kid to pull himself together.

While we wait, in the background we hear the ambient sounds of a certain open mic night gradually drowning out the whimpers of the kid.

> FRANCIS (in the background): Great. The piece is titled, "Fucked in the Ass by the Star-Crossed Prophylactadon".

Still in the background, Francis clears his throat in exactly the same way he did when we visited this scene in-person.

CUT TO: OPEN MIC NIGHT

With an assist from the miracle of narratorial time dilation, allow me to spend this pregnant pause mentioning that as we saw earlier, Tony, sloppy drunk, sits by himself at a table. This time, though, we can't help but notice (perhaps it's the camera angle) the dangling shirt sleeve that has not been cut off and sewed. This is not, as you are probably thinking, an objective correlative for Francis's falling down on the job of looking after the platonic love of his life. It's just a matter of the shirt belonging to Francis.

Anyway, do with this information about a shirt shared between two men who deeply love each other what you will. Just so you know, the shirt is neither a basic plaid button-down like the one Jack Twist borrowed from Ennis in *Brokeback Mountain,* nor is it made of blue denim like the one Ennis finds covering the plaid button-down on a hanger in the dead love of his life's closet in the scene making your narrator cry like a baby as we speak. (And if you're not crying, what's wrong with you?)

Still, the shirt Tony's wearing, a baby blue men's Henley with a total of three optional buttons on it, would serve perfectly well as the objective correlative for Tony and Francis's heartbreaking love for each other.

If it seems like I'm stalling right now, it's because I am. I don't want Tony to go, and it hurts me to have to tell you here in this stretched-out pregnant pause before "god tosses" that "icy clot of hard luck" that on this final visit to this open mic night, we also notice that there is something very different about this fall of Tony's off the wagon. He looks somehow beyond ever pulling himself back together again. Sadly, we watch Tony fading even further as Francis recites the poem (in its entirety, not because I'm stalling but because of how proud Tony was of Francis for crushing it like he did).

> FRANCIS: God tosses one icy clot of hard luck. Levels all his terrible lizards, who spend, oh, only about 65 thousand millenniums [sic] pooling the essence of their incredible collective penchant for being royally screwed in one fell swoop. Brewing, brewing, brewing in a soup of gooey crude oil in its greatest role as a broken prophylactic waiting untold

eons to happen. Waiting, waiting, waiting. Dying, dying, dying to rise once more so they can go bust all over again and then, Eureka, up this unlucky muck is sucked through the human straw and is brought to the processing plant and then off it goes to the prophylactic factory, which spits out this little one and a half inch by one and a half inch package of cold-blooded petroleum-based doom—brings to pass the second coming of the star-crossed prophylactadon that springs from its flat and kinda krinkly little Pandora's box and figuratively speaking proceeds to fuck me all Jurassically [sic] in the ass before dying a gooey death in my hand.

We hear Francis's face banging against the microphone. It stops.

FRANCIS: No petroleum jelly.

More banging. It stops.

FRANCIS: No sweet nothings.

More banging. It stops.

FRANCIS: Definitely no reach-around.

More banging. It stops.

FRANCIS: Just a good…hard…unlucky…fucking in the ass.

More banging. It stops. Francis has seamlessly converted his bending over into a triumphant bow without the crowd knowing it at first. Tony's wild one-handed clapping isn't giving everyone the hint until it is and everyone's giving Francis a big two-handed hand.

THIRTY-TWO

Francis and Tony sleep on their bench, Tony lying across Francis's lap, calling to mind the pieta scene where I prepared you for this one. Both aging young men have developed a snore by this last of Tony's nights on this earth.

Among other things, this improbable capstone pose presses home the hand some smartass cosmic choreographer has had in managing the decades'-long dance of life that Francis and Tony have spent together.

FADE TO: ALMOST DAWN

Angle on Francis. Deep in thought, he watches the approaching break of day. Of all things, he is wondering if "the second coming of the star-crossed prophylactadon" makes any sense in light of the prophylactadon's probably not ever having had a first coming.

The day breaks so beautifully as to erase not only these troubling thoughts but also the utter absence of Robin's beauty in everything in the world.

Francis nudges Tony, who's still lying across his lap.

> FRANCIS: Tony. If you could have Robin back for one hour, what would you do?

Tony doesn't answer. Francis nudges him, nudges him again, and, panicking, again.

Long shot of a sobbing Francis rocking Tony's body as he sits there in their favorite spot.

FADE TO: BUSY SIDEWALK – DAY

Close-up of Francis's hopeless face as he crawls along on all fours.

Welcome to Act 3.

The camera pulls back to take in Francis's sad progress among his gaping, path-clearing, two-legged fellow pedestrians.

> IMAGINARY FRANCIS (V.O.): Yes. That is me looking for Tony. I want to say to him, "So, Francis. You have just helped kill your best friend. How are you supposed to ask him what brand of rotgut you should use to kill yourself for helping to kill your own best friend?"

Francis arrives at a liquor store. An exiting customer holds the door open for him as he crawls in.

CUT TO: PARK – DAY

Francis sits alone on his and Tony's bench. He drains the last of a bottle of rotgut.

FADE TO: PARK – NIGHT

Francis lies passed out on the bench he now has all to himself.

> IMAGINARY FRANCIS (V.O.): There I am one, maybe two, days away from succumbing to the rotgut. That terrible stench you smell is the already dead monkey that Lewis brought to life in me many years earlier.

Weirdly, we hear the sweet humming of the disco song that Francis and Tony and for a very short time Robin jazzercised to.

THIRTY-THREE

We are back, of course, at Francis's bench. Only this time we are focused on the unbelievably sweet face of Henry, like the Navigator, Francis's nine-and-a-half-year-old boy.

He is afflicted with the facial tic that goes off periodically as he sweetly hums the so familiar disco song we weirdly heard at the very end of the last chapter. A cowlick adds somehow to Henry's sweetness.

The camera pulls back. We see that Henry is sitting on one end of Francis's bench. Francis sleeps face-up with his head in Henry's lap. Henry strokes his father's hair as he hums. If you look closely you can see Henry sweetly suppressing all but the teeny tiniest bit of his whole-body desire to jazzercise along with the catchy song.

> IMAGINARY FRANCIS (V.O.): That there is the unbelievably sweet thing I helped Robin contaminate with the filthy genes she got from one of her mother's rapists, which, of course, I don't know about yet at the time of this moment's unfolding. He has recently escaped his horrible foster home. With the help of various homeless people and a couple of others, and with his "really good sense of direction," and thanks to a lapse perhaps on the part of who or whatever's in charge of hauling me back to where this ridiculous existence of mine all got started, he has made his way to me.

Henry looks lovingly at something in the hand not being used to stroke Francis's hair. It's the snapshot of Francis and Tony with their arms around Robin.

> IMAGINARY FRANCIS (V.O.): It's like I thought. Even a picture of Robin keeps getting more and more beautiful by the minute.

Angle on Francis. He opens his eyes, as if his own imaginary

Voice Over has just woken him up. He does his best to orient himself as he listens to Henry hum a sweet, slow, very well-rehearsed version of his and Tony's old song, "I Will Survive" by Gloria Gaynor.

I have understandably been resistant to giving the universe the satisfaction of making light of our story and the mortal coil it plays out in by inserting a mysterious serendipity like this that's so on the nose. It does make you wonder, though, how the universe chose "I Will Survive" over "Stayin' Alive" or "Don't Leave Me This Way" or "The Love I Lost" or "Last Dance" or "Bad Luck". A less editorializing universe would have gone with something more neutral like "Boogie Oogie Oogie" or maybe "Ring My Bell".

Anyway, back at the mortal coil, Henry notices that his dad has awakened. He stops his humming, smiles at him, twitches.

FRANCIS: Who are you?

HENRY: I'm Henry, like the Navigator. I know who you are. You're Francis, like the Talking Mule. You're my dad. I knew I could find you.

Henry smiles, twitches. Francis stares at Henry, who after a moment, twitches again.

HENRY: Where's Uncle Tony?

Francis is not ready yet for this question.

FRANCIS: I don't know. Where's your mom?

HENRY: You don't have to say "your" mom. You can just say "mom".

FRANCIS: Where's mom?

HENRY: I don't know. We have to go look for her.

Francis very shakily manages to sit up.

FRANCIS: How could you not know where your— how could you not know where mom is?

Henry twitches.

> HENRY: When I was six and a half, she got in bad
> trouble for being a lady of the evening and they put
> her in jail and took me away from her and put me in a
> foster home.

I know. I know. I can hear all you brake-pumpers and
slammers out there doing your own editorializing about how
too far a bridge it is to get from the Robin we all know to the
incarcerated scarlet woman Henry just made mention of.

What can I say but get over it? It's been two and a half
millenniums since none other than Sophocles taught us all
how much like child's play it is for the cosmos to drop us in
the worst lot in life possible. And by Sophocles I do mean the
ancient Greek dramatist whose name to this day means
"Smart Glory", and who was the winner of no fewer than 18
City Dionysias, the Pulitzer Prizes for Drama of their day.

And anyway, how about we think about Francis right now,
who's got so much to absorb there in the hollowed-out shell
of himself.

For a while as his dad fights off a sob, we watch Henry
exercise his inherited way of sitting motionlessly next to a
loved one on a bench as the world goes by.

> FRANCIS: How did you know where to find me?

> HENRY: Just before I was taken away from mom,
> she and I came here to look for you and Tony, but we
> couldn't find you.

Francis buries his face in his hands while we recall Robin's
sobbing as she knocked on the door of the apartment Henry's
father and uncle of course had vacated bare moments before
they needed to be there for Robin and the sweet little boy
about to be taken away from each other.

> HENRY: Luckily I have a really good sense of
> direction. I found the bench on the first try.

Francis sits motionlessly next to his new loved one. Henry

puts his arm around him. The two sit like this a long time.

FRANCIS: What is that terrible smell?

HENRY: I think I might have accidentally stepped in dog poop.

Francis just nods.

THIRTY-FOUR

At a mom and pop diner, Francis sits at a table looking at the snapshot of him and Tony and Robin. He drinks from a bottle wrapped in a paper bag.

Henry sits before a plate with a once-bitten-into hamburger and a pile of french fries on it. If anything, his cowlick has become even more pronounced since we saw it last. Now he also has mustard on his face. He twitches.

We watch him try to get catchup to come out of the bottle he is shaking over his fries. He gives up without much of a fight, puts the cap back on the bottle and puts the bottle back where it was. He takes up the saltshaker. When he goes to sprinkle a little salt on the fries, the booby-trapped top comes off, leaving salt all over everything.

> HENRY: Whoops.

Angle on Francis, who has just watched this stroke of bad luck muck up this plain old everyday undertaking of his son's.

Angle back on Henry, who takes one end of a french fry between two fingers, shakes off a lot of the salt, eats the fry. He makes a face that says, "Not too bad." Then he twitches.

> HENRY: Dad. Right after lunch, can we start looking for mom?

Francis takes a drink, stares at Henry a moment. Henry twitches.

> FRANCIS: Did mom ever tell you how you came to be born?

> HENRY: No.

> FRANCIS: Never mentioned anything about a broken rubber?

> HENRY: What's a rubber?

Francis takes a long drink.

> FRANCIS: A rubber, Henry, is a metaphor for just how little stands between us and the bad things that happen to us.

> HENRY: Oh.

Taken aback a little by this understated reaction, Francis stares at Henry long enough for several twitches to happen.

> FRANCIS: How long has your face been doing that?

> HENRY: A pretty long time.

> FRANCIS: Can you make it stop? I think I'm catching it.

> HENRY: No.

Francis watches Henry. He twitches again, then suddenly begins making monkey faces. Puzzled, Francis looks over his shoulder in the direction of the faces Henry is making.

Angle on a baby aping Henry's monkey faces. Of course that is Lewis trying to reach Francis through Henry. Francis goes back to looking at Henry, who smiles at his dad, twitches.

> HENRY: I really love babies. Mom told me you're really good at making babies laugh.

Henry eats another very salty french fry. Francis takes a napkin, licks it, reaches over and wipes the mustard off Henry's cheek.

> HENRY: Thanks, dad. Dad, do you want my pickle?

> FRANCIS: No thanks.

> HENRY: Dad. Can we go look for mom now?

> FRANCIS: Sure, Henry. But we should probably do something about that tic first.

> HENRY: Ok.

THIRTY-FIVE

Francis knocks on a door. He looks at Henry standing next to him, licks two fingers, and tamps down Henry's cowlick. Henry twitches.

FRANCIS: What's mom like?

HENRY: She's really really pretty and nice. And sometimes she's funny.

Francis nods.

HENRY: Dad. Can I tell you something?

FRANCIS: Shoot.

HENRY: Well. You really shouldn't step on the cracks.

Francis looks puzzled.

HENRY: When you're walking on the sidewalk.

Francis figures out what Henry's driving at.

FRANCIS: You mean because it breaks your mother's back?

Henry shakes his head yes, twitches.

FRANCIS: That's a superstition.

HENRY: I know. But just in case.

Francis thinks this over for a moment.

FRANCIS: Ok.

Henry's dad chooses not to mention that stepping on a line is also said to break a mother's spine. There's no way he's going to make Henry think about all the lines he's probably stepped on in his itinerant little life.

Paul answers the door.

FADE TO: LIVING ROOM

Henry sits alone on the sofa. Paul sits nearby in an armchair.

Francis stands next to Paul. The two men watch Henry periodically twitch. His cowlick has already popped back up.

You will be pleased in a moment to see that against all odds, Paul has found almost all the powers of speech that his so untimely rogue stroke took away from him. And no, this is not your narrator serving you a sweet little morsel of food for the positive thought that things lost can be found after all. Paul, as his homonymic ties to a certain feeling of gloom testify to, is sitting there assuming the role of the exception that proves the rule that the universe is hardly in the business of giving back what it goes to all the trouble of taking from us.

Focus on Paul squeezing his blue rubber stroke victim's ball as he watches Henry sit on the sofa sweetly holding together the bundle of adjustments to injuries and slaps added to injuries that he is. For all the world the rubber ball looks like the world we'd all like to crush sometimes for the cruelty it is capable of.

Angle on Henry. He twitches.

> FRANCIS: Can you use hypnosis or something?

> PAUL: Let's just start by talking. How does that sound?

> HENRY: Pretty good. But me and my dad need to go soon. We have to find my mom.

Angle on Francis, who looks pretty green around the gills.

> FRANCIS: Got anything to drink, Paul?

> PAUL: All out.

> FRANCIS: I'll be right back.

We and Henry really don't want Francis to go.

CUT TO: SIDEWALK

On a curb outside a convenience store, Francis sits drinking heavily from a bottle.

If the real Francis were watching us watch him drinking like that at a time like this, he'd say, "I have not had a single drink since the one I am having right there."

Francis drunkenly and not successfully at all is trying to miss the cracks and the lines on his way back to Paul's place.

> IMAGINARY FRANCIS (V.O.): While I'm accidentally rebreaking and rebreaking and rebreaking my poor mother's long-ago broken back when I'm not busy rebreaking her spine, my poor son Henry, like the Navigator, is telling Paul all about the life he has navigated so far. It is filled with such wonders as an unbelievably fucked up foster dad who spent the last third of Henry's life so far doing the most evil things to him.

We watch Francis badly navigate his own life for half a block or so.

CUT TO: BATHROOM – NIGHT

Henry sits in the tub taking a bath. Still periodically twitching, he sweetly hums a certain disco song as we look at all the scars on his poor torso.

Henry would not let his dad see him without his shirt on. Later, Henry will tell Francis that what hurt him the most about those scars his foster dad left all over him when he was drunk is that they meant he couldn't grow up to be an artist's model like Francis. The facial tic hurts him for the same reason.

CUT TO: BEDROOM – NIGHT

Lost in thought, Francis lies face-up in his bed. Henry lies face-up right next to him.

> HENRY: Dad. Can we go look for mom in the morning?

> FRANCIS: Henry. You don't ever really find the things you lose.

HENRY: I found you.

Francis rolls over on his side so Henry can roll over on his side in the opposite direction and see the picture of fatherly sternness Francis has summoned to his face.

FRANCIS: Don't sass me, boy.

The straight face Henry is trying to keep between twitches breaks into a wide smile.

HENRY: Good one, dad.

FRANCIS: Thanks.

Francis smiles, rolls back over. Henry also rolls back over.

FRANCIS: Truth is, Henry, you found the shell of me.

HENRY: Dad.

FRANCIS: Yes.

HENRY: You can feel free to just call me son if it's easier than saying Henry.

FRANCIS: Thanks, son. I think I'll do that.

Henry smiles. Angle on Tony's empty bed.

HENRY: Dad. Where's Uncle Tony?

FRANCIS: Uncle Tony's dead, son.

Angle on Henry. He breaks down and cries. Francis collects Henry into his arms.

We see Tony's empty bed again, and we see the blood-testing instruments and the alarm clock on the bedside table.

THIRTY-SIX

Tony lies dead on his and Francis's bench. Francis has left Lewis's monkey on his chest so he won't be all alone. A newspaper covers Tony's face so people will think this is someone just catching some shuteye before some next shoe drops on an obviously hard life.

CUT TO: ART STUDIO

Naked and sobbing, Francis lies prone before a roomful of uncomfortable art students drowning the rest of the universe out with the untold thousands of words their pictures are worth.

CUT TO: HARDWARE STORE

Francis buys a round-pointed shovel.

CUT TO: SIDEWALK – DAY

Francis puts our teeth on edge with the sheet-steel shovel blade he's dragging along the concrete behind him as he makes his way back to Tony.

CUT TO: PARK – SUNSET

Having violently plunged the blade of the now standing shovel in a patch of Mother Earth beside him, Francis, crying like a baby, sits on one end of his and Tony's bench, Tony's head in his lap. Lewis's monkey still sits on Tony's still unmoving chest.

Francis is being made angrier and angrier by the pallor and the algor and the livor and the rigor mortis relentlessly impressing upon him that the universe isn't nearly done with Tony yet.

At one point it will occur to Francis to snicker for Tony's left arm that the world doesn't have available anymore for subjecting to the four mortises and the four stages of decomposition.

At another point Francis will practically hear Paul in his ear telling him he is projecting his blame for Tony's death on everything he can lay his eyes on. Of course Paul is too wise and nice a guy to say such a thing to Francis at a time like this. So you tell me who's posing as Paul in our hero's ear.

The newspaper, sickeningly reminiscent of the wind-tossed litter that broke Tony and Francis's backs a couple of years earlier, still covers Tony's face.

FADE TO: SUNRISE

Nothing beautiful about it.

FADE TO: BENCH – MORNING

Dirty from burying Tony, Francis sits alone. No Tony. No Lewis's monkey. Just a terrible hangover he's too numb to feel and the shovel planted to the hilt in the ground again beside him.

Who cares what offshoots of our 4,125-year-old original human laws Francis broke in keeping the world's nose out of and its grubby and bloodied hands off this returning of Tony to the dust he came from?

For a while we watch Francis wait for the denial or even the bargaining or even the depression stage of the complex grieving process to come and save him from the shock of a Tonyless existence stretching out there like a miserable 40-year wilderness a lost soul doesn't come out of alive.

Want to see a sweet memory that Francis stumbled upon at about mid-afternoon?

FADE TO: PARK – EVENING

Francis and Tony, tipsy, sit on their bench wearing party hats on the day Francis turned the same age his dad was when he killed himself for killing Lewis.

> TONY: Francis. Do you think baptism covers all your body parts?
>
> FRANCIS: You hope your arm's waiting for you up there in heaven?

TONY: That would be nice.

FRANCIS: Hope it didn't go to hell for jerking off a minor.

Tony smiles.

TONY: It was just a first offense.

FRANCIS: Maybe it's in lim-bo.

Tony smiles. So does Francis. They take a drink from their respective bottles.

TONY: Francis.

FRANCIS: Yeah, Tony.

TONY: Would you say you love me?

FRANCIS: I love you.

TONY: No, I mean, do you love me?

Francis looks at Tony very tenderly.

FRANCIS: You know how much I love Robin, right?

Tony nods.

FRANCIS: I think I might love you more than that.

Tony smiles, looks away. Francis puts his arm around him.

THIRTY-SEVEN

It is the morning of the second day of the rest of Francis and Henry's life together. Francis sits up in bed watching his son sleep free of his twitching.

Francis nudges Henry, who opens his eyes, smiles at his dad.

FRANCIS: Let's go look for mom.

HENRY: Ok, dad.

Henry smiles more widely, undergoes his first twitch of the day.

CUT TO: PAUL'S PLACE

Francis and Henry stand together in Paul's living room. In body language, Francis is screaming for a drink, a really stiff one.

He tamps down Henry's cowlick and spit cleans the egg left on his face from breakfast.

HENRY: Thanks.

Henry twitches. Paul enters the room, walks with a slight favoring of his right side up to Francis and gives him a handful of money.

FRANCIS: Thanks, Paul.

PAUL: All I ask for in return is a kiss from Robin when you bring her back.

Francis hugs Paul. In better days, he would have joked about his grossly underestimating the cost of one of Robin's kisses.

They unclinch. Henry steps in and gives Paul a hug.

It is all Francis can do to keep from crying over Paul's purchase of a kiss from Robin reminding him of the act of vandalism poor Robin committed against herself by becoming a lady of the evening.

CUT TO: FLOWER SHOP – MORNING

Francis and Henry exit, Henry holding a bouquet. He sneezes.

CUT TO: PARK – MORNING

Henry cries, his face buried in his dad's midsection. Francis is doing his best not to cry. We see that he and Henry are standing next to where Tony is buried. It is near a tree not far from the bench.

The flowers Henry was holding have joined several older bouquets on the ground.

To this day it helps Francis a little to think of Lewis's monkey keeping Tony company. It helps him, too, to think that Tony might have found his arm after all. And maybe his healthy pancreas. What helps most, though, is to think of Tony up there playing Baloo to Lewis's Mowgli and King Louis.

Henry stops crying.

> HENRY: Dad. If we ever get separated, let's always meet at Tony's bench.

> FRANCIS: We're never going to get separated, son.

> HENRY: I know. But just in case.

Henry looks up at Francis, twitches.

> FRANCIS: Ok.

With a finger and thumb, Francis clears the snot from Henry's nose.

> HENRY: Thanks, dad.

THIRTY-EIGHT

Henry and Francis sit side-by-side on a Greyhound bus. Focus on the warmed-over death that Francis is looking like.

> IMAGINARY FRANCIS (V.O.): There I am in the most dire need of my morning shot of embalming fluid as Henry and I head to San Francisco.

Angle on Henry, who looks up and smiles at Francis till he twitches. Francis smiles queasily back at him.

> IMAGINARY FRANCIS (V.O.): There I am doing my terrible best to not let Henry see how angry I am at god and the cosmos over the cruel stupid irony that after all that effort I put into killing myself with rotgut, it is the lack of rotgut that is going to kill me. I'm not crazy either about the irony of my orphaning Henry in my Herculean attempt to be there for him.

Another Greyhound goes racing in the opposite direction past Francis and Henry's bus.

> IMAGINARY FRANCIS (V.O.): On top of everything else, of course, I am assuming that this trip to the Golden City is coinciding once again with Robin's leaving it to come look for me (and Tony). I think I'll let your extra omniscient narrator handle the commentary that this situation calls for.

> YOUR NARRATOR (obviously no need to say V.O.): In case you haven't noticed, our story is loaded with weirdly verisimilitudinous flirtations with a little big toe's-worth of dip outside the bounds of verisimilitude. We have all seen life give the lie to that thing about lightning never striking in the same place twice (if you haven't, well, good for you, but you're probably lying to yourself). In other words, we've seen fox be taken twice or more in the same snare. We all know all too well that the opportunity to

be screwed by our own stabs at avoiding a good screwing seldom knocks twice--because it's so busy knocking three and four and five and a thousand or more times. So Francis and his imaginary counterpart were not being paranoid or defeatist at all in thinking that every single bus that blew by them in the exact opposite direction of their bus had Henry's mom and the female love of Francis's life on it. Enough said.

OK, one more thing, maybe two. You yourselves at this point of the story should not rule out the possibility of god and the cosmos beating the astronomical odds against Robin and Francis swapping places again in their efforts to fix the tearing of them apart. And for the record, if you're feeling put upon by the unlikely ironies and coincidences our story has been familiarizing you with, get over it. You haven't even been asked yet to suspend your disbelief with respect to how mysteriously sinister god and the cosmos can be.

FADE TO: BUS STATION – EVENING

Francis and Henry step off the bus, Francis with a satchel in one hand and his smiling son in the other.

CUT TO: CHEAP HOTEL

They share the room's queen-size bed. The room clock flashes 12 over and over and over while you're flashing back to the Cinderella Inn and then to that thing I just said about coincidences.

CUT TO: SIDEWALK – MORNING

Avoiding both cracks and lines, Francis and an unsmiling Henry, hand-in-hand, make their way up a foggy San Francisco hill.

CUT TO: HOUSEFRONT – MORNING

They stand looking at the large house that looms before them.

FRANCIS: You sure this is your grandma's place?

HENRY: Yes.

FRANCIS: You've been here how many times in your whole life?

HENRY: Two.

FRANCIS: And you're sure this is the place?

HENRY: I have a really good sense of direction.

FRANCIS: Ok.

Francis tamps down Henry's cowlick, spit cleans the breakfast from Henry's face again.

HENRY: Dad. I don't think she likes me very much.

Francis, puzzled, puts his arm around his son.

HENRY: She has a lot of bad scars on her face.

It takes Francis a minute to absorb this first real inkling of how much more horrible Robin's demons are than he thought.

CUT TO: LIVING ROOM

Looking too small, Henry sits by himself in one lonely armchair. Francis does the same in another.

Across a small rug from them, Robin's mother sits austerely on one side of a loveseat. Her name is Jewel. Her face is terribly disfigured.

JEWEL (to Henry): You found your dad.

Henry shakes his head yes, twitches.

JEWEL: At one time, I was my daddy's girl.

Henry smiles weakly, twitches.

JEWEL: Do you know who your mom's dad is?

Henry shakes his head no.

JEWEL: Neither do I. I don't know if it's the first one who raped me or the second or the third. I'm reasonably sure, though, that it wasn't the one who sodomized me.

Jewel looks over at Francis, who wants badly to cry and otherwise fall apart but doesn't let himself do so in front of his son.

JEWEL: Robin didn't tell you how she came to be born?

Francis shakes his head no, looks at Henry, whose lip is trembling. With a visible effort, Francis keeps himself pulled together.

FRANCIS: Can you tell us where we can find Robin?

Jewel seems to ignore the question as she sits a moment absorbed in thought.

JEWEL: I have no family history of breast cancer.

Francis and Henry are first puzzled then terrified by this announcement.

JEWEL: So Robin must have gotten those genes from her dad.

Henry buckles.

FRANCIS: Robin has breast cancer?

JEWEL: That's hard to say. She doesn't have breasts anymore. My dad paid to have them removed. And for the chemotherapy. And the radiation.

Henry falls utterly apart. His shoulders rise and fall as he silently sobs. The sobbing also jostles his cowlick.

Angle on Francis as he watches Henry.

IMAGINARY FRANCIS (V.O.): That is my love for Henry growing to almost unmanageable proportions. It's a good thing his mother and his little Uncle Lewis and his Uncle Tony stretched out my capacity for love so much. Don't ask me why my parental instincts didn't scream at me to go hold Henry at the first sign of his crying instead of make note of how much I loved him. It's just one of those things.

Again Francis calls on his inner Hercules.

FRANCIS: Is Robin going to be ok?

JEWEL: Yes. I believe so.

FRANCIS: Do you know where we can find her?

JEWEL: No.

FRANCIS: Does your dad?

JEWEL: He's never even met her.

Jewel and Francis watch Henry sob. Francis gets up, goes over and lifts him into his arms. Unexpectedly, he then goes over with Henry and sits next to Jewel on the loveseat.

FRANCIS: I'm so sorry those guys did what they did to you.

Jewel is fighting back tears.

JEWEL: I never had her baptized.

FRANCIS: Henry and I'll take care of that.

THIRTY-NINE

Francis and Henry, wrung out, sit next to each other on a
park bench. Henry has stopped sobbing, but his nose still
runs. His dad takes care of it with a pinch from a thumb and a
first finger and a deft little flick of the snot onto the park
lawn, a maneuver that reinforces all we already know about
how Francis is taking to fatherhood. It goes without saying
that Henry twitches periodically in the exchange to follow.

> HENRY: Dad. Have you been baptized?

> FRANCIS: Yes. Have you?

> HENRY: Yes.

Francis keeps it to himself as he curses the men of god who
must have missed a spot when they dipped him and Henry
into the holy water to cleanse away the sin they have been
paying for through the nose without any letup to speak of.
Francis sits there knowing pretty much how Achilles must
have felt.

> FRANCIS: Son. I need to go ask your foster mom
> and dad if they know how to find mom.

> HENRY: I know.

> FRANCIS: You don't have to go to their house with
> me. You can wait for me somewhere safe while I go
> talk to them.

> HENRY: You don't want to just call? I know my
> foster mom's phone number by heart.

> FRANCIS: I think I need to be there in-person.

> HENRY: Ok.

Francis clears the snot again from Henry's nose, puts his arm
around his bravely not un-smiling son.

> IMAGINARY FRANCIS (V.O.): There I am
> devoting what's left of my life to shielding Henry

from all the bad things that happen to us.

Angle on a honeybee that busily bee-dances its way a la a certain slip of windborne litter and not wholly unlike a certain clot of hard luck toward our hero and the ward he has just pledged to protect. Of all the near infinite number of places available to it, it lands on Henry's neck, then heads down under his collar.

> IMAGINARY FRANCIS (V.O.): That is a honeybee breaching my shield like it was nothing. It is just about to give its little life to pay me back for taking not one but two men of god's names in vain and to make Henry keep paying I guess for the smudge of sin that was still left on his person after his baptism was over. On sort of the upside it has also given its busy little life to reinforce the point your narrator recently made about how mysteriously sinister god and the cosmos can be. A lot for even a busy customer like a honeybee to get done in one fell swoop.

The bee stings Henry.

> HENRY: Ouch. Ouch. Ouch.

Henry looks worriedly at Francis looking worriedly at him.

> HENRY: Oh no. Dad, I'm very allergic to bees.

This time Francis's parental instincts kick in instantly, only to find, though, that the target of their incitement into action is already halfway to the hospital with Henry in his arms along with the whole lifelong struggle he comes with.

CUT TO: HOSPITAL WAITING ROOM

A wreck, Francis sits waiting for word about Henry's condition.

He is still violently torn between telling god what a sick son of a bitch he is and offering god any body part of his he wants in exchange for not taking Henry away from him.

Angle on a policeman, who enters the room, spots Francis, and walks up to him with an unmistakable firmness of purpose.

COP: You the guy that brought in Tony?

FRANCIS: Tony?

COP: The kid with the bee sting. The doctor was under the impression his name is Henry, but the kid keeps insisting his name is Tony S. Bench and that I should go ask the guy who brought him in if I didn't believe him.

Francis tries hiding his surprise and his fatherly pride over the chip off his block's ingeniousness.

FRANCIS: Tony S. Bench? Never heard of him. I brought in my brother Lewis. He was in a car accident.

COP: So you don't know Tony or Henry or whatever the kid's name is?

FRANCIS: No. Is he ok?

COP: Oh, he's great. If you don't count the nasty facial tic and all the burn and knife scars some sick son of a bitch left all over the poor kid.

Francis shakes his head with genuine sadness.

COP: Hope your brother's ok.

FRANCIS: It's not looking good.

COP: I'm sorry to hear that, sir. I'll keep him in my prayers.

Francis thanks the officer for his kindness and then bites his lip instead of giving him a citizen's tip about a certain cosmic crime boss he ought to be taking a good look at instead of saying prayers to him.

FORTY

A bus takes Francis back to Tony's bench as per the plan. At this point you'd be well within your rights as a dear reader to half expect to finally have to suspend your disbelief because the bus suddenly becomes involved in a fiery survivorless head-on collision with a bus that's got Henry's mother in it.

Do not worry. Such an awful *deus ex machina*'s not in the offing, though it's true that almost if not all bets are obviously off in a story where a hero's son is stung by a bee he happens to be deathly allergic to within seconds of his dad's promising with all his heart to protect him.

It's really something the strains that credulity can undergo in a stupid universe where the teeny and tiniest trace amounts of star-gotten iron and nickel and cobalt can make such powerful tragedy and near tragedy magnets out of us.

CUT TO: PARK – NIGHT

Francis sits on Tony's bench waiting for Henry. Let's let imaginary Francis briefly weigh in on the whole bee thing.

> IMAGINARY FRANCIS (V.O.): Do not get me started on the cruelty of one little honeybee popping the bubble of the future I was beginning to hope for with my son and my honeybunch. What ruthless muse is out there inspiring the Author of All Things to enlist one of the birds' fellow symbolizers of the making of babies to take my baby away?

The real Francis just sits there shaking his head.

FADE TO: PARK – MORNING

Francis hasn't budged.

That sound you hear is him trying to eke some comfort out of listening to Tony play air guitar to Lewis's delight up there in heaven. It is actually managing to sooth the savage inner she bear that god has aroused in him with his constant harassing of his child.

Francis even half smiles. If Tony were there, he'd give him an easy one. He'd say, "Hey, Tony. You have reached the very top of the stairway to heaven. Both your arms are attached again to your body. What Led Zeppelin song do you choose for shredding on your electric air guitar?"

Tony brings the other half of Francis's smile to his face thanks to how doubtlessly he would have said something like, "Gosh, Francis, I can't think of one."

FADE TO: PARK – AFTERNOON

Paul delivers lunch and a bottle of water to Francis.

FADE TO: PARK – EARLY EVENING

Francis sits tight.

> IMAGINARY FRANCIS (V.O.): There I am taking another short break from worrying myself to death about Henry and Robin. I am daydreaming about the first and now only time I ever saw Robin's beautiful bare breasts.

Close-up of Francis's face as he visualizes Robin's beautiful onetime breasts.

> IMAGINARY FRANCIS (V.O.): I'm not going to lie to you. I'm going to miss them terribly. You saw them. They were perfect. A million times better than the ones I drew on Venus de Milo back in the sixth grade. Remember that? When you were told to remember how much I love breasts?

FADE TO: PARK – EVENING

Angle on Francis's face. He smiles. We see Henry, like the Navigator, coming his way.

FORTY-ONE

Francis and Henry stand together in Paul's living room. Paul enters the room with a whiff of déjà vu and hands Francis more money.

> FRANCIS: Thanks, Paul.

> PAUL: Now it's two kisses. You better find her soon or she and I are going to become an item.

This, of course, is Paul trying to bring the inner monkey in Francis back to life. It is not working. Francis is too busy knuckling and buckling and bearing down with regard to his job as Henry's guardian.

CUT TO: HIGHWAY – NIGHT

A bus takes Francis and Henry back to San Francisco.

> IMAGINARY FRANCIS (V.O.): As it turns out, Henry, like the Navigator, AKA Tony S. Bench, escaped the hospital no problem. Found a homeless guy he used to know who found a lady who knew a guy whose half-brother's dad or something like that was going in Henry's direction. So the guy drives Henry to our park, and then before Henry gets out of the car, he makes Henry jerk him off for his trouble.

Francis looks out the window at all the darkness. And yes, the darkness is meant to call all the world's awfulness to mind.

Henry sleeps leaned up against Francis on the crowded bus.

> IMAGINARY FRANCIS (V.O.): Henry says, without the least little bit of sympathy-grubbing, that the hand job's not the worst thing that's ever happened to him. I'd have sworn to god that I would never let anything like that happen to my son again, but you've seen how good I am at protecting the ones I love.

Angle on Francis's sad face.

> IMAGINARY FRANCIS (V.O.): That's god's big gift to guardianship you're looking at right there. I personally can't help wondering what it is that god is god's gift to.

FADE TO: HIGHWAY – NIGHT

The bus plunges into the darkness on its way to San Francisco.

FADE TO: BUS STATION

The bus pulls in.

CUT TO: LIBRARY – DAY

Francis sits next to Henry in a reading area.

> FRANCIS: Son. Do not talk to any strangers.

> HENRY: Ok, dad.

> FRANCIS: Do not talk to anyone you may have become acquainted with at some earlier point in your life.

> HENRY: Ok, dad.

> FRANCIS: Keep a sharp lookout for bees.

> HENRY: Ok, dad.

> FRANCIS: And flying monkey wrenches. And comets. And loved ones with contagious viruses. And cars going in reverse.

> HENRY: Ok, dad.

Close-up of Francis's reluctance to leave Henry by himself. You might think Francis was trying to be funny with that weird litany of potential dangers, but he wasn't.

Angle on Henry, who's clearly picking up on Francis's seriousness. He twitches under his dad's concerned look which just intensifies the concern and brings on another twitch.

FRANCIS: Are there any dangers I'm forgetting?

HENRY: Well. I'm pretty allergic to other insect bites too.

FRANCIS: Ok. Just avoid all insects.

HENRY: Ok, dad. Dad. Sometimes I almost choke to death on my food.

FRANCIS: Do not put anything in your mouth while I am gone.

HENRY: Ok, dad. Also, dogs like to bite me. And I sleepwalk a lot. That's pretty dangerous. Oh yeah, and I think the cops are probably looking for me.

FRANCIS: Ok, Henry. Look—

With his finger, Francis outlines a box around Henry.

FRANCIS: Think of this as an invisible protective box, a padded one with a lifetime supply of enriched oxygen in it and a double if not a triple redundancy's-worth of safeguards against collapsing built into the design. Can you do that?

HENRY: I can.

FRANCIS: Excellent. Now just stay inside the box. Do not fall asleep. Do not let any dogs in. Do not answer the door if someone tries to deliver Chinese or any other kind of take-out to you. I don't care how good it smells. There's no door on the box anyway. Just sit tight in there and think happy thoughts about mom and or navigating till I get back.

HENRY: Dad.

FRANCIS: What, son?

HENRY: I'm sorry, but I have a really bad fear of enclosed places. Could you make the box a little bigger? And maybe put a door on it if I promise not to open it.

(Little Side Note: Later Francis will find out that Henry's foster dad used to lock him into enclosed spaces for no reason if you don't count his knowing that his foster son was deathly afraid of enclosed spaces.)

Francis rushes to fix the protective casing for Henry. He even gives him a window. Henry smiles, twitches, then looks seriously at Francis.

> HENRY: Dad. Watch out for my foster dad. He's very mean.
>
> FRANCIS: Son. It's your foster dad who needs to watch out for me.

FORTY-TWO

A taxi drops Francis off in a residential area.

CUT TO: DOORSTEP

Francis knocks on the door. In a moment, Henry's foster mom opens it.

> FRANCIS: I'm Henry's dad. I have Henry. We need to know where we can find Henry's mom.

Henry's foster mom is taken aback. Henry's scary-looking foster dad arrives at the door, moves his wife aside.

> FOSTER DAD: Who are you?

Later, Francis will be very grateful that he didn't say something like "Your worst nightmare" or "I am the can of whoop-ass you ordered."

What Francis did say was nothing. He was too instantly dumbstruck by how much Henry's foster dad stood there embodying all the harms that are constantly being thrown at us.

Francis punches him in the face. He recovers easily, launches an assault that sends the two off the porch and into the small yard.

A la Cool Hand Luke but without the gloves on, Francis futilely keeps fighting back as Henry's foster dad delivers him a brutal beating. Coincidentally, Henry's foster dad is roughly the size of Dragline, as played by George Kennedy.

> IMAGINARY FRANCIS (V.O.): There I am beginning to suspect that a funny, tenderhearted diabetic with one arm and a set of well-formed buttocks might not have been the best training partner for a showdown with the forces of wanton harm.

After absorbing many many blows, Francis goes down and cannot get back up. Henry's foster dad kicks him a couple times for good measure, then walks back into his house.

144

IMAGINARY FRANCIS (V.O.): Embodied Forces of Harm, one. Francis's Inner Hercules, zero.

After a few moments, Francis manages to stand up, albeit with a wobble, and albeit on all fours. He crawls across the yard toward the front door.

IMAGINARY FRANCIS (V.O.): That giddyup and quirt-smack you heard is my Inner Hercules riding me into a re-match.

CUT TO: FRANCIS

Lying half incapacitated again in the middle of Henry's former front yard, our hero is being kicked in the groin by Henry's foster dad.

IMAGINARY FRANCIS (V.O.): For those of you who can't bear to watch, I am being kicked repeatedly in the nuts and thereabouts by the embodiment of all the harms that god and the cosmos are always throwing at us.

Henry's foster dad stops the kicking. We watch him walk again into Henry's old residence.

IMAGINARY FRANCIS (V.O.): Embodied Forces of Harm, two. Francis's Inner Hercules, still zero.

Angle on Francis, who now has a goofy smile on his bloodied face as he lies crumpled on the ground.

IMAGINARY FRANCIS (V.O.): Yes. There I am a little punch drunk. Yes. I have been beaten silly not once but two times without much of a recovery period between them. But the reason for the goofy smile is that into my head I have just had beaten a very valuable and pleasing revelation—one that I guess I'd experienced at least subconsciously a long time ago. And the revelation is this: It is not with your inner Hercules that you fight back at a heartless god and cosmos. It is with your inner monkey.

Francis rolls over onto his back and looks up at the sky.

IMAGINARY FRANCIS (V.O.): When god starts tossing harms our way, we have to just throw handfuls of our own dookie back at him. We have to jerk off in his general direction. When the going gets tough, ladies and gentlemen, the truly tough just stick a finger in their anus for no apparent reason and make monkey faces, maybe while doing the world-famous Monkey Dance and belting out the lyrics "ooh ah ah, ooh ah ah."

Reverse angle on Francis. From god's POV we see that a new kind of smile is now playing across his face.

IMAGINARY FRANCIS (V.O.): That new shit-eating grin you see right there was inspired by my realizing that my inner monkey was not dead after all. It was only mostly dead. All the Forces of Harm have managed to accomplish with this latest kicking of my ass is the waking up of their worst nightmare. And in case you're wondering, no. I can't now account for that terrible stench you smelled back in whatever act and chapter that was when my real self thought my inner monkey was a rotting corpse. Take it up with your narrator, who'll probably point out how often a live monkey smells like shit.

We see Henry's foster mom exit the house, walk up to and kneel beside Francis.

IMAGINARY FRANCIS (V.O.): This is Henry's foster mom telling me that Robin secretly calls her every few weeks to ask about how Henry's doing. She tells me that Robin, she thinks, has been sick lately—which of course I already knew—and, most importantly, that she's pretty sure Robin works at a flower shop in the Upper Haight District, of all places for a man and a boy to go looking for the love of their life.

FORTY-THREE

Still somewhat punch drunk, Francis sits with a very concerned-looking Henry on a bench outside the library.

Before we move on, let me attend to a little narratorial housekeeping:

1. Flash back a skosh if you will to the plot twist of Francis epiphanicly figuring out that the best defense against all the monkeying that god or whatever you want to call it does with us is a hysterically offensive monkeying right back with him or it. Now flash forward a bare handful of frames to the moment when a certain bench warmer on the victorious Forces of Harm team does god's bidding by sending Francis on a guilt trip for the heart-blossoming gratitude he feels toward the poor example of a mom figure who failed so miserably to protect Henry from the sick monster she was so likely failing miserably to protect herself from as well as to send Francis on a guilt trip within a guilt trip for feeling guilty about feeling grateful to this poor woman who has just braved who knows what dangers (we know, actually) to cough up the rough whereabouts of Robin. Of course, within this guilt trip within a guilt trip Francis soon finds himself zipping along on a third and final guilt trip over his own pattern of failing miserably to protect the ones unlucky enough to find themselves in his care. Anyway, where all the guilt-tripping takes our super punch and love-drunk and also aha moment-inspired hero is to the spectacle of his lying there in Henry's onetime front yard wearing a virtual hair shirt while madly scratching his armpits like a kid making like a monkey making like The King singing, "I'm itchin' like a man in a fuzzy tree." Francis of course is putting some extra juice in it for Lewis and Tony up there. Henry's former neighbors, the ones who've been religiously keeping their nose out of other people's business, keep doing so when like a stuck record Francis sings, "I can't seem to stand on my own two feet. No, really, I can't seem to stand on my own

two feet. I'm not kidding over here, I can't seem to stand on my own two feet."

2. Let's hear it for the objectively heckuva job Imaginary Francis did with the Voice Over in that last chapter.

3. A big thank you is probably in order to god/the cosmos for refraining from taking a wrecking or a cannon ball or a cluster bomb or other menacing projectile to Henry's invisible protective box.

4. Everybody knows monkeys smell bad enough to be mistaken for something rotting. I give you the commonplace "like stink on a monkey" if you don't believe me.

5. Speaking of monkeys, keep in mind when you judge Francis on his performance in taking on the Forces of Harm's Goliath figure that the monkey of hard liquor that's been on his back probably took a lot out of him.

Anyway, we're back now at the reading area of the library. Francis is still somewhat punch drunk, given that magically no time has actually passed since we last saw him and a "concerned-looking" Henry sitting there in the aftermath of Francis's hard-bought new outlook on life.

> HENRY: I'm sorry he beat you up.

> FRANCIS: Beat me up? What are you talking about, son? You should have seen me clobbering him in the shoe repeatedly and mercilessly with my nuts.

Henry's not quite sure how to react as his dad really believably winces and whimpers a little at the self-inflicted mention of the nuts-kicking he just underwent.

> FRANCIS: You know, son. I hate like heck to second-guess a street-smart guy like myself, but in perfect 20/15 hindsight going on 20/10, maybe I didn't need to clobber your foster dad in the steel-toed shoe with my nuts quite so hard.

Henry begins to laugh.

FRANCIS: You hear that? That's the pounding of your dad's nuts. They are throbbing so hard that they're creating more pounding which is creating more throbbing which is creating more pounding and so on. What if the twin sources of our nuclear family are melting down in a chain reaction that won't stop till my poor nuts are in China? God only knows what those people will do with them down there.

Francis takes Henry's face in his hands, looks earnestly into his laughing son's eyes. Waits for a twitch that doesn't quite come for some reason.

FRANCIS: Run for your life, son. Seriously, save yourself. But before you go, do you have any ice I could borrow? A ten-pound bag should do it. Preferably the crushed kind, so I can scoop it into my underwear, which I might have accidentally pooped in a little during a certain kicking of the shit out of me.

Francis winces twice.

FRANCIS: Note to Francis: Do not say "pound" right now, and definitely do not say "crushed."

Francis winces twice again.

Henry now cries with laughter. Francis watches him, very pleased. He must and does admit he has to hand it to god for making nuts so funny.

IMAGINARY FRANCIS (V.O.): There I am performing a thorough exam on Henry's inner monkey. As you can see, it passes with flying colors.

Francis watches Henry's laughter play itself out.

FRANCIS: Guess what, son.

HENRY: What, dad?

FRANCIS: What do you mean, what? I'm pretty sure I just heard your dad tell you to guess what. Do not make him tell you again.

Henry keeps a barely straight face.

HENRY: Ok. Let me see. Let me see.

Henry scratches his head in the area of his cowlick, rubs his chin.

FRANCIS: Go ahead and stand up so you can scratch your ass if you need to. I could do it for you if you don't have enough hands.

Henry stands. Francis scratches his ass while Henry scratches his head and rubs his chin.

HENRY: Got it.

Henry sits, lets the suspense build a little.

FRANCIS: Well?

HENRY: Here's my guess: Your POUNDING and CRUSHED nuts are making you cranky.

Francis makes a big show of wincing twice while inside he says to himself, "Oh my god, this is the beginning of a beautiful friendship."

FRANCIS: Well played, son. But your guess is incorrect.

HENRY: Want me to guess again?

FRANCIS: For the love of god, no. If you would be so kind as to give your dad a very very gentle drumroll so as to spare his nuts any percussive and or concussive consequences that might ripple out in their direction, I will give you the correct guess.

Henry gives his dad a very very gentle drumroll.

FRANCIS: Your foster mom told me that mom works in a flower shop.

Henry's face and whole body take on all the most joyful qualities of a shop full of flowers.

HENRY: Oh my god, dad. Mom loves flowers.

Francis smiles. We do too as the memory of all the beautiful bouquets on Robin's and Tom's kitchen table comes flooding back like the last ten years never happened.

FRANCIS: The shop is in the Haight district.

HENRY: I bet I know exactly where it is.

FORTY-FOUR

A taxi unloads Francis and Henry on a sidewalk and then takes off.

Across the street we see the flower shop that Henry, like the Navigator, has found on his first try.

Angle on Francis, who primps a little before submitting his battered appearance to Henry's inspection.

FRANCIS: How do I look?

Henry winces, twitches.

FRANCIS: That's what I thought.

HENRY: At least you don't have a tic.

He twitches again. Tenderly, Francis tamps down Henry's cowlick, clears the snot from his nose.

FRANCIS: You know, son. I've been meaning to tell you. Your tic is really growing on me. I think you should think about keeping it.

HENRY: Ok, dad. I'll think about it.

FRANCIS: That's my boy. Hey Henry, why did the capon cross the road?

HENRY: What's a capon?

FRANCIS: A capon, son, is a chicken whose poor nuts have been impounded.

Henry smiles.

FRANCIS: And he crossed the road so he could make sure the road-crossing chickling he loves so much wasn't struck by a city bus or a garbage truck or a runaway cable car just before a certain mother hen got her chickling back and vice versa.

HENRY: Think we should use the crosswalk up there at the stop sign?

152

FRANCIS: I can't wait that long.

Francis stops everything he's doing, looks both ways, listens, steps out into the street and begins jaywalking with the chickling.

FRANCIS: After this one time, son, absolutely no more jaywalking.

HENRY: Ok, dad.

Francis and Henry manage to avoid all buses and trucks and cable cars while crossing the street. They enter the flower shop.

CUT TO: FRANCIS AND HENRY

They stand just inside the door, a smiling lady looking at them from behind the shop's checkout counter.

FRANCIS: What the hell did you do to mom, Henry? She looks way different from when I knew her.

HENRY: I don't think that's her, dad.

LADY (to Henry): You must be Henry, like the Navigator?

Henry smiles, shakes his head yes.

LADY (to Francis): You must be Francis.

HENRY: Like the Talking Mule.

The lady smiles. Francis smiles.

LADY: Robin broke down a little when she saw you two across the street. She's in that room right there.

Angle on a closed door.

LADY: She should be out in a minute.

Angle on Francis.

FRANCIS: I can't wait that long.

Francis looks at Henry.

FRANCIS: Ready?

Henry wants to be ready, but instead he breaks down and cries, buries his face in Francis's midsection.

Francis lifts Henry up into his arms. He walks up to the closed door, opens it, steps inside the room.

Close-up of Francis's face. On it we see the same unforgettable look we saw when he laid eyes on Robin for the first time.

> IMAGINARY FRANCIS (V.O.): It's exactly like I suspected. Robin had gotten unbelievably more beautiful. Way more beautiful even than how much more beautiful she had gotten in my imagination or in the picture of her over all those years.

Robin sits among a profusion of flowers. Her hair is very short. Her face shows signs of her battle with cancer and with life in general. Through her tears, she smiles widely at Francis and Henry.

FORTY-FIVE

On a park bench, Francis sits with his arm around Robin, who sits with her arm around Henry. They all look every bit as content as you'd expect. Actually, they look a lot more content even than that. A lot more.

> IMAGINARY FRANCIS (V.O.): Look at us. Three hopeless sitting ducks in our greatest role as a happy family.

Henry twitches, goes back to simply smiling.

> IMAGINARY FRANCIS (V.O.): God and your extra omniscient narrator only know what slings and arrows and big-ass flying monkey wrenches will be thrown at us. Of course, I mean in addition to the daggers that will pierce Robin's heart soon when she finds out about Tony and about poor Henry's life since she last saw him. Weirdly, I could almost kiss Henry's foster mom for sparing Robin some of these piercings for a while by lying to her about how Henry was doing. It would be more like a peck than a kiss.

CUT TO: ROBIN'S PLACE – DAY

With Henry bringing up the rear, Francis carries Robin over the threshold of her tiny apartment.

Bouquets blanket Robin's kitchen table.

Angle on Francis. He looks at Robin and she smiles at him.

CUT TO: SOFA

Smiling, Francis sits with his arm around Robin, who also smiles. His arm has been stone dead for a while now, but that's not why he's not moving it.

Henry expertly runs through Francis and Tony's, and for a short time Robin's, jazzercise routine. We ourselves can sing "I will survive" along with Henry's moves if we so choose.

> IMAGINARY FRANCIS (V.O.): No matter what hits

us, though, no matter what glancing or full-on harms breach our latex-thin figurative prophylactic shield or our even thinner invisible protective family box, we're going to do our best to keep our inner monkeys alive and kicking.

Angle on Robin, who's now sedentarily doing the routine along with Henry. Francis calls Tony to mind as he also sits there doing the routine but minus the arm that's gone dead, as mentioned.

> IMAGINARY FRANCIS (V.O.): We don't need to go looking for Robin's breasts. Or Henry's innocence. Or even for Tony. Or for Lewis and his monkey. Or for my clean record. Or Robin's. Or for those ten years lost all because of one busted rubber.

Angle on Henry again.

> IMAGINARY FRANCIS (V.O.): I would like to go back in story time right now and not say anything bad about that busted rubber I have to thank for this stupid universe outdoing itself in producing another loved one for me as sweet and beautiful as Lewis and Tony and Robin.

We help Imaginary Francis get his imaginary wish by erasing all memory of that bad thing he didn't say about the busted rubber.

Henry finishes his workout, counts the pulses in his left wrist.

> IMAGINARY FRANCIS (V.O.): Since it looks like artist's modeling isn't in the cards for Henry, I will need to look for a different line of work that he can dream of taking up just like his dad. Who knows? Maybe I'll become a very successful businessman like my dad after all.

Angle on Francis.

> IMAGINARY FRANCIS (V.O.): I don't know, though. Watching me in a sitting position like my

calling and life in general have so often plopped me in for long stretches of time, I have to wonder if whole-body repetitive motionlessness hasn't taken too big a toll on my person for me to go out there and knock myself out making the world my lobster or my oyster or both. Maybe Robin can help me enter an exciting new career as a flower shop delivery boy paving the way for the son following (very cautiously) in his father's footsteps by way of taking full and complete advantage of his superpower of navigation.

Robin looks over at Francis with a certain kind of love in her eyes.

IMAGINARY FRANCIS (V.O.): And by the way, if and when my poor nuts recover, I personally plan repeatedly to seek out comfort in the arms of Robin. If you know what I mean.

FORTY-SIX

Here is one last little bonus chapter before we go our separate ways.

Robin and Francis lie face-up together in Robin's small bed. Henry sleeps like the thousand-word picture of peacefulness between them.

Next to the bed, tacked to the wall, is the sketch Tom drew of Francis sitting on a piano bench motionlessly throwing himself at Robin.

If we had more time, I would attempt to express to you how inexpressibly good it feels to Francis to be lying there in bed with Robin and Henry. I'll just let a close-up of Francis's face do the talking.

> ROBIN: I miss Tony.
>
> FRANCIS: Me too.

They think about Tony a moment.

> FRANCIS: Robin. I had sex with Tony.
>
> ROBIN: That's ok. I had sex with everyone else.

The room is quiet for a moment.

> FRANCIS: Um, yeah. Speaking of that, I kinda pimped you out to my friend Paul. You owe him two kisses.
>
> ROBIN: Will pecks on the cheek do the trick?
>
> FRANCIS: I think so.

More quiet.

> FRANCIS: Robin. I'm an ex-con.
>
> ROBIN: Me too.
>
> FRANCIS: I think I might also be an alcoholic.
>
> ROBIN: We'll work through that.

Francis props his head up in one hand, looks earnestly at Robin.

FRANCIS: Robin. I'm a mime.

Robin is crestfallen.

ROBIN: Oh no, Francis. They're never going to let us have Henry if they know you're a mime.

FRANCIS: Well. I know *my* lips are sealed.

ROBIN: That might be a giveaway.

FRANCIS: Oh, right.

Francis goes back to looking up at the ceiling.

FRANCIS: Anyway, good luck keeping Henry, like the Navigator, away from his mom and dad.

Robin and Francis smile as they think about their son. Francis becomes serious.

FRANCIS: Robin. Henry's perfect.

Robin mirrors Francis's seriousness.

ROBIN: I know.

More quiet.

FRANCIS: Robin.

ROBIN: Yes.

FRANCIS: I have loved you so much.

Robin breaks down, begins quietly weeping. Francis strokes her short hair.

IMAGINARY FRANCIS (V.O.): She won't be ready for a while, but when I'm double sure she is, one day I will tease Robin. I will shake my fist at the heavens and I will say, "Why? Why, god, why? Why did it have to be the breasts? Why couldn't it have been the arms like what happened to Venus de Milo?" Playfully Robin will hit me, probably on the chest with one of her beautiful fists, and I will say, "I repeat, why couldn't it have been the arms?" And Robin will laugh. And Henry will laugh. And I will laugh, because really, you know, what else can we do?

FADE OUT

www.ingramcontent.com/pod-product-compliance
Lightning Source LLC
Chambersburg PA
CBHW050348030726
47503CB00008B/2668